The old man retrieved the gun and hung it on the bedpost, as Clint had requested.

"What about my rig?" the Gunsmith asked.

"The lock is still on the door," the sheriff said. "They didn't get inside. In fact, it don't even look like they tried."

"Then what did they want?" Clint asked.

"I'm afraid you're not going to like this," the sheriff said. "We got the story from the liveryman."

"Where was he?"

"He came back after you got hit," the sheriff said, "and saw . . . the rest."

"What rest?" Clint asked. "Damn it, what's going on?"

"Your horse, son," the doctor said.

"What about him?" Clint asked. "What about Duke?"

The doctor looked at the sheriff, who looked down at the Gunsmith and said, "He's gone, Adams. They took your horse . . ."

Don't miss any of the lusty, hard-riding action in the new Charter Western series, THE GUNSMITH:

THE GUNSMITH #1: MACKLIN'S WOMEN
THE GUNSMITH #2: THE CHINESE GUNMEN
THE GUNSMITH #3: THE WOMAN HUNT
THE GUNSMITH #4: THE GUNS OF ABILENE
THE GUNSMITH #5: THREE GUNS FOR GLORY
THE GUNSMITH #6: LEADTOWN
THE GUNSMITH #7: THE LONGHORN WAR
THE GUNSMITH #8: QUANAH'S REVENGE
THE GUNSMITH #9: HEAVYWEIGHT GUN
THE GUNSMITH #10: NEW ORLEANS FIRE
THE GUNSMITH #11: ONE-HANDED GUN
THE GUNSMITH #12: THE CANADIAN PAYROLL
THE GUNSMITH #13: DRAW TO AN INSIDE DEATH
THE GUNSMITH #14: DEAD MAN'S HAND
THE GUNSMITH #15: BANDIT GOLD
THE GUNSMITH #16: BUCKSKINS AND SIX-GUNS
THE GUNSMITH #17: SILVER WAR
THE GUNSMITH #18: HIGH NOON AT LANCASTER
THE GUNSMITH #19: BANDIDO BLOOD
THE GUNSMITH #20: THE DODGE CITY GANG
THE GUNSMITH #21: SASQUATCH HUNT
THE GUNSMITH #22: BULLETS AND BALLOTS
THE GUNSMITH #23: THE RIVERBOAT GANG
THE GUNSMITH #24: KILLER GRIZZLY
THE GUNSMITH #25: NORTH OF THE BORDER
THE GUNSMITH #26: EAGLE'S GAP
THE GUNSMITH #27: CHINATOWN HELL

And coming next month:

THE GUNSMITH #29: WILDCAT ROUNDUP

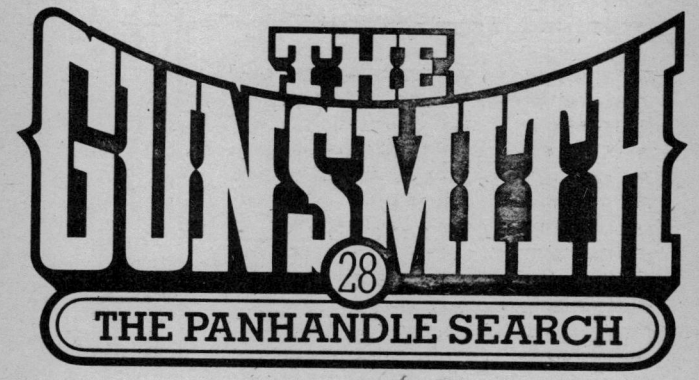

THE PANHANDLE SEARCH

J.R. ROBERTS

CHARTER BOOKS, NEW YORK

THE GUNSMITH #28: THE PANHANDLE SEARCH

A Charter Book / published by arrangement with
the author

PRINTING HISTORY
Charter Original/May 1984

All rights reserved.
Copyright © 1984 by J.R. Roberts
This book may not be reproduced in whole
or in part, by mimeograph or any other means,
without permission. For information address:
The Berkley Publishing Group, 200 Madison Avenue,
New York, New York 10016

ISBN: 0-441-30900-3

Charter Books are published by The Berkley Publishing Group,
200 Madison Avenue, New York, New York 10016.
PRINTED IN THE UNITED STATES OF AMERICA

Dedication

To Dirty Gordy

ONE

Little Creek, Wyoming had turned out to be a bonanza for the Gunsmith. In less than a week, his wallet's size had doubled. Not only did it seem like every gun in town had suddenly malfunctioned, but he couldn't seem to draw a losing hand in poker, even if he wanted to—and he didn't. Between his gunsmithing fees and his poker winnings, Christmas had definitely come early. On top of all that, he'd spent six days in town without once hearing the words "the Gunsmith" used in any other way than to describe the work he was doing.

The topper was the girl that he was in bed with at the moment. She was a young and lovely and extremely energetic blonde whose freshness and honesty had been most welcome after all the traveling he'd done during the past few weeks.

But even with all of this, six days in one place was still too much for a man stricken with wanderlust to take, and it was time to leave.

As the morning light filled his hotel room, Clint Adams

moved one leg, preparing to leave the bed without waking up Brenda Mills, the blonde lying beside him, but that was not to be. As soon as his foot touched the floor, Brenda's blue eyes opened and fastened on him.

"Where do you think you're going?" she asked.

"I told you last night—"

"—that you were leaving in the morning," she finished. "What did you think I was going to do, cling to you and beg you not to go? Even if it's only been six days, Clint, you should know me better than that."

She was right, of course. For a girl just shy of her twenty-first birthday, she was remarkably mature, and it was foolish of him to think about trying to sneak out on her.

It seemed even more foolish when she pushed herself up to a seated position, and her bare breasts came into view. They were lovely, coral-tipped mounds of smooth, ivory flesh, and he felt a phantom itching in his hands, as he had since the first time he had seen them naked.

"You're right, of course," he said, putting his foot back on the bed and turning toward her.

He palmed her breasts and the nipples hardened beneath his touch. He leaned forward to take the right one between his teeth, flicking it with his tongue at the same time, and she moaned and eased down onto her back, taking him with her.

Clint mounted her eagerly—and for the last time, he thought, not without a touch of sadness—and slid easily into her slick, warm cavern.

"Oh, God, yes, you bastard," she said. "Fuck me and leave me, right?"

"Brenda—"

"Shut up," she said. "Don't waste any of that marvelous energy talking."

He obliged, directing himself to the task of bringing her to

THE PANHANDLE SEARCH 3

a final, shattering climax, one that would stay with her for a long time to come. . . .

She watched him dress afterward and asked, "Do you think you'll ever come back this way?"

How many times had he heard that question? "It's possible, Brenda, but—"

"I'm not asking you to promise anything, damn it," she snapped. "When are you gonna get it into your head that I'm not some lovesick young girl looking for promises?"

"I'm sorry," he said.

"You should be," she said, watching him strap on his gun. She turned her head, hoping that he wouldn't see the moistness in her eyes. *Get out*, she shouted at him silently, *before I make a fool of myself*.

"Good-bye, Brenda," he said. He approached the bed and kissed her on the forehead, while she kept her face averted.

"Good-bye, Clint," she said. "Take care of yourself. If you're ever in San Francisco, look me up."

"You'll make it," he told her. "I know you will."

"I know it too," she said.

It was only her iron will that kept the first tear from rolling down her cheek until she heard the door close behind him.

It was the first of many.

Clint walked down to the lobby and settled his bill, and while he was paying up, a large, broad-shouldered man in his late fifties entered and strode to the desk.

"I'm looking for a man named Adams," he told the clerk.

"I'm Adams," Clint said, before the clerk could reply. "What can I do for you?"

The man turned to face Clint and, although he was not quite as tall as the Gunsmith, he was able to create the illusion that he was looking down at him.

"I want to buy your horse, Adams," the man said. "Name your price."

This was far from the first offer Clint'd had for Duke, but it seemed to be the most serious.

"Sorry," he said, "I'm not interested in selling." He started to leave but the man caught his left arm in a surprisingly powerful grip.

"I'm not accustomed to taking no for an answer, Adams," the man said. "Do you know who I am?"

"No," Clint said, staring the man in the eyes, "but I know where you'll be if you don't take your hand off my arm."

The man blinked twice, very slowly, then loosened his grip and dropped his hand to his side.

"My name is Chandler, Adams. They call me 'Moose' Chandler. You've heard of me, I know."

Indeed, the Gunsmith had heard of Moose Chandler. He had one of the largest spreads in Texas, and was best known for raising quality horses. However, there was no reason to let Chandler know this.

"Sorry," Clint said, "never heard of you."

He started to leave again, and this time Chandler called after him without grabbing his arm.

"Adams, I want that animal," he said. "I'll pay you twice as much as I've ever paid for a horse before."

Clint kept walking.

"Three times as much!"

"Not for ten times the amount," Clint called back. "Good-bye, Mr. Chandler."

Clint left the hotel, half expecting Chandler to come rushing out after him, but the rancher had apparently given up.

He walked to the livery stable, leaving the incident behind him.

As he entered the stable he noticed that the liveryman was

THE PANHANDLE SEARCH

not around, but that was okay. He preferred to saddle Duke himself, anyway. After that, he'd hitch up the team and be on his way.

"Steady, big boy," he said, approaching Duke's stall, "it's just me."

"No, it ain't," a voice said from behind him.

Clint turned slowly, since he didn't know whether or not the owner of the voice was holding a gun on him. If he was, a quick move might cause him to pull the trigger prematurely.

There were two of them, and neither one of them had his gun out, although they seemed ready to produce them at a moment's notice.

"Who might you fellows be?"

"We're just a couple of cowboys interested in your horse," the man on his right said. Clint noticed that the man was right-handed, but that the cuff of his left shirt-sleeve was empty. He had an arm, but his hand was missing. The other man had two hands, one of which was hovering near his gun. They looked more like a couple of hardcases than a couple of cowboys.

"I've had one offer for my horse today, friend," Clint said, "and I didn't like that one any more than I like this one."

"That's a shame," the one-handed man said, "because that means that we'll have to take him from you."

"You're welcome to try," Clint said. He felt confident that he would be able to outdraw both men, but he wasn't as confident that he would be able to do anything other than kill them.

Why were people always pushing him, even when they didn't know who he was?

Or did they?

"Whenever you're ready to take him from me," Clint said, "you can give it a try."

"Oh, we're ready," the man said, "ain't we, Floyd?"

For a moment, Clint thought that the man was talking to his partner, but too late he realized that one-hand was speaking to someone behind him. There were three of them, and he had realized it too late to do him any good.

He was in the act of turning when something struck him a solid blow on the back of the head, and he felt himself falling into a deep, black well.

His last conscious thought was that he hoped this well had a bottom.

TWO

When Clint woke up he was surprised to find that he was not on the livery floor. He was in a bed, and he had a pounding headache.

"How are you doing?" a voice asked.

Moving only his eyes, he sought out the source of the question. There was a man standing to the right of the bed, looking down at him, an elderly man with a white mustache and watery eyes.

"What?"

"How are you feeling?"

"I've got a headache."

"Thank God that's all you have, young fella," the man said.

"Who are you?"

"I'm Doctor Sanders," the man said. "I'm the one who kept your head from falling apart when they brought you in here."

Clint contemplated trying to move, then decided against it.

"How bad?"

"Not that bad, really," the doctor said. "Turn your head to the left, just a little."

Clint obeyed, and a bell went off inside his skull. He rested his left cheek on the pillow and the doctor bent over him. The man's body odor was oppressive, and it struck Clint that a doctor should take better care of himself.

"Not too bad, at all," the old man said again, "as long as you don't move around for a while."

The doctor straightened up and Clint frowned, trying to remember what happened. He was in the livery stable, saddling Duke, when two men braced him. No, three men. One came from behind and hit him.

"What did I lose?" he asked.

"Some blood, not much—"

"No, I mean, was I robbed? Did they take my money?"

"You'll have to talk to the sheriff about that," the old man said.

"Get him for me, will you, doc?"

"Sure," the doctor said. "There's a girl waiting outside to see you. She can stay with you while I go get the sheriff."

"Fine."

As the doctor left Clint heard him speak to someone in the hall, and then the door closed and Brenda was beside the bed.

"How are you?" she asked.

"Fine, fine," Clint said. "I've got a bump on my head, that's all."

"That's good," she said, taking his hand. "I looked out the window of your hotel room and saw them carrying you over here, so I rushed over. I—" she began, but her voice caught in her throat and she had to swallow to clear it. "I thought you were dead."

"Do me a favor," he said, to take her mind off of it. "Check my pockets, will you? I'd like to see if they took my money."

"Sure," she said.

She walked to the chair where his clothes were draped and went through his pockets. She took what money there was back to the bed so he could count it, and it was all there.

"They didn't take my money," he said, puzzled. "What the hell did they want?"

What was it they were saying just before he got hit? He couldn't remember. The incidents just prior to his getting hit were still too fuzzy in his mind.

Brenda returned the money to his pockets, then brought a chair over to the bed so she could sit beside him.

"Can I get you anything?"

"A drink," he said.

She grinned and said, "That's what doc said you'd ask for. He said I'm not to give you one."

Clint finally felt that he could move his hands, and he reached up to touch his head. There was a bandage on the back, and he traced his fingers over it without putting any pressure. There was enough throbbing behind his eyes without adding to it himself.

He closed his eyes and must have dozed off, because when he opened them the doctor and a man wearing a tin star on his chest were standing there looking down at him. Brenda was gone.

"Sheriff," he said.

He'd met the sheriff once, the day he had ridden in and, thankfully, had not had the opportunity or necessity to talk to the man again . . . until now.

"Mr. Adams," the lawman said. "Glad to see you're still in one piece. Can you tell me what happened?"

"It's still very hazy, Sheriff," Clint said.

"It'll come back, son," the doctor said. "Just don't try to force it."

"There were two men," Clint went on, "or three, I think.

Someone hit me from behind. . . ."

"That much is obvious," the doctor said, "and a damned good clout they gave you, too. You must have a hard head."

"What did they get from me?" Clint asked. "I've still got all my money. My gun—" he said, suddenly feeling his stomach lurch. Had they taken his modified Colt?

"Your gun is here," the doctor said. "I put it in the top drawer of the chest."

"Could you get it out, doc?" Clint asked.

"Sure," the doctor said, "but you won't be needing it here."

"I'd just feel better if you would hang it on the bedpost," Clint said.

The doctor looked at the sheriff, who shrugged his indifference. The old man retrieved the gun and hung it on the bedpost, as Clint had requested.

"What about my rig?" he asked.

"The lock is still on the door," the sheriff said. "They didn't get inside. In fact, it don't even look like they tried."

"Then what did they want?" Clint asked.

"I'm afraid you're not going to like this," the sheriff said. "We got the story from the liveryman."

"Where was he?"

"He came back after you got hit," the sheriff said, "and saw . . . the rest."

"What rest?" Clint asked. "Damn it, what's going on?"

"Your horse, son," the doctor said.

"What about him?" Clint asked. "What about Duke?"

The doctor looked at the sheriff, who looked down at the Gunsmith and said, "He's gone, Adams. They took your horse."

THREE

"Lester, the fella who runs the livery, says that they knew what they were doing," the sheriff said. "They looked like they'd handled troublesome horses before. They blindfolded him, hobbled him, and led him out."

It all came back to him in a rush, now. The men in the livery said they were interested in Duke, and it was too much of a coincidence to believe that they had no connection with Moose Chandler.

"Chandler," he said, aloud.

"What?" the sheriff asked.

"Moose Chandler," Clint said. "Is he still in town?"

"I don't know," the lawman said, "I'd have to check with the hotel. Why?"

"He wanted to buy my horse," Clint said. "Stopped me in the lobby when I was on my way out. He got very upset when I refused his offer."

"What are you gettin' at?"

"I think he had his men waiting for me in the livery," Clint said, "just in case I refused to sell."

"You think Moose Chandler had his men take your horse from you?"

"It's too much of a coincidence to be any other way," Clint said.

"Chandler's a big-shot rancher," the sheriff reminded Clint. "You sayin' he stole your horse?"

"That's what I'm saying."

"You'd have to have more proof than what you're givin' me," the sheriff said, "before I could take any action."

"That's okay, Sheriff," the Gunsmith said. "I don't need you to take any action. I'll take my own action."

"You gonna go after him?"

"He won't be that hard to find," Clint said. "I'll just go to Texas, to his ranch, and get my horse back."

"You can do what you want," the lawman said, "as long as you don't cause any trouble in my town."

"Sure," Clint said, "I can see how you don't like trouble in your town, Sheriff."

"I told you I can't take no action without proof," the sheriff said. "I can find out if he left yet, and maybe question him—"

"Don't bother, Sheriff," Clint said. "He's gone. He's well on his way back to Texas. I'll find him."

"Not for a while, you won't," the doctor said. "You got a nice cut on the back of your head that's got to heal yet. You'll have to sit tight for a few days—"

"Don't worry, doc," Clint said. "I'm not in a big hurry. I know just where Chandler's heading, and he'll be there waiting for me when I get there."

There was a cold look in Clint's eyes that neither the sheriff, the doctor, nor Brenda failed to notice, and they were all chilled by it.

Clint closed his eyes, hoping all three of them would think he was going to sleep and leave. He thought about Duke, about how many times the big black horse had saved his bacon. Now it was his turn. He'd make sure he was healed up first, before going after him. Chandler was a horseman, and Duke was in no physical danger. Both Chandler and Duke were headed for Texas, so there was no problem about locating them. Chandler had to feel that he was untouchable once he got back to his ranch, but he was obviously ignorant of whose horse he had stolen.

The Gunsmith intended to make him well aware.

FOUR

Clint allowed himself two days in his hotel room before he finally got restless and left it, against the doctor's wishes.

"I won't take the responsibility if that cut opens up again," the doctor said.

"Don't worry, doc," Clint said. "You've been paid. I'll be responsible for my own head."

Clint had breakfast in the hotel dining room, then sat back and tried to relax over a second pot of coffee. Relaxing had been something he'd been unable to do, even while lying in bed. Although he knew that Duke was in no physical danger, he itched to go after the big black and get him back. He knew, however, that he'd be in for a war once he got to Texas, when he tried to take the horse back from Moose Chandler, so he had to be in top physical condition himself.

And he'd need a horse, one he could count on. That was his first order of the day, after breakfast. Clint needed a horse he could have confidence in, and after so many years of riding Duke, that was not going to be an easy thing to find.

After he finished his second pot of coffee, he left the hotel and walked over to the livery stable. When the liveryman,

Lester, saw him enter, he stopped what he was doing and stared nervously at the Gunsmith.

"Jeez, mister, I'm sorry—" he began, but Clint cut him off before he could go further.

"Forget it, Lester," he said. "I wouldn't expect you to go up against three men to save someone else's horse."

"Well, I'll tell you, mister, if I was gonna do it, it would of been for your horse. That was—I mean, that's some animal."

"Tell me what happened, Lester," Clint said. "Did they hurt the horse? Did they give any indication that they intended to hurt him."

"Not until he took a piece out of one of them," the liveryman said, with a grin.

"He bit one of them?"

"Took a chunk out of one of their hands when they was trying to blindfold him," Lester said.

Clint couldn't help but grin. "Did they know what they were doing?"

"They was horsemen, all right," Lester said. "When he bit that one fella, he pulled his gun as if to shoot the horse, but the other two stopped him. They said the boss wouldn't like it."

"Which one was bitten?"

"The one with one eye," Lester said. He laughed and added, "Now he's got one hand, too."

"Serves him right," Clint said. "Did you notice if it was his gun hand?"

"Naw," Lester said. "He was bit on his other hand."

Clint nodded and asked, "You got any horses I can look at?"

Shaking his head, Lester said, "I got some in the back, but nothing like that black of yours."

"Let's take a look at them."

He followed Lester out back, where there was a corral with six or seven horses.

"Mostly they're horses I had to keep when somebody didn't pay their bill, or when somebody got killed."

"Will you give me a good price?" Clint asked, although he didn't see one he especially liked.

"Mister, your horse was stolen out of my livery," Lester said, "and he was the best piece of horseflesh I ever seen. If you need one of these horses to go after him, you can have your pick."

"Thanks," Clint said. "Let me look at them for a few minutes."

"Sure," Lester said. He had a big nob of an Adam's apple that bobbed up and down when he spoke, and it was his only distinguishing feature. "I got some work inside. Let me know what you decide."

Clint had intended to go into the corral and look more closely at the six or seven horses, but he decided against it. He could see that there weren't any that he'd care to take a trip to Texas on. For the most part they were too old and well worn.

Satisfied that he couldn't find what he wanted there, he turned and went back into the livery.

"Pick one?"

Clint shook his head and said, "None of them is good enough."

"I was afraid of that."

"Do you know anyone who might be able to sell me a horse?" Clint asked.

"There are a couple of ranches nearby that might have some for sale," Lester said. He told Clint where they were, and who owned them.

"Nothing else in town?"

Shaking his head Lester said, "Not that I know of, mister.

THE PANHANDLE SEARCH

Your best bet is to try those ranches."

"I will. What happened to my saddle? Did they take that, too?" he asked.

"No sir," Lester said. "I've got that right here."

"Would you pick the best horse out of that lot and saddle it up for me? I'll use it to ride out to these ranches."

"Sure, mister."

"Thanks. I'll be back in a little while."

Clint left the livery and walked over to the sheriff's office, where he found the lawman seated behind his desk.

"What can I do for you, Adams?" the sheriff asked. "As I understand it, you shouldn't even be up and around."

"I was just wondering if you had found out anything about Moose Chandler."

"Nothing that will help you," the sheriff said. "He left town the same day you spoke to him."

"Right after his men took my horse."

"Look, Adams—"

"I know. I don't have enough proof for you," Clint said, "but I've got enough for me."

"What are you planning to do now?" the sheriff asked as Clint started for the door.

"Right now I'm going to see a man about a horse," Clint said.

FIVE

Clint stopped at the first ranch Lester had told him about and found nothing there that he could use. He was on his way to the second one when he heard the first shot.

He launched himself from the saddle out of pure instinct, hit the ground with his shoulder and rolled. He heard the second shot while he was rolling, and heard the horse he'd been riding cry out. When he stopped rolling he had his gun in his hand and was looking around for the source of the shots.

When the third shot sounded, Clint took the only cover that was available, which was the carcass of the now dead horse.

He flattened himself against the belly of the still warm animal and gradually became aware of the sound of hoofbeats as they faded away.

He stood up, holstered his gun and stared down at the dead animal. Moose Chandler was making a habit out of taking his horses. Clint had no doubt that the man who had done the shooting was one of Chandler's, probably left behind to make

THE PANHANDLE SEARCH 19

sure that Clint didn't follow. Either he'd had instructions not to kill, or he had botched the job. What Clint couldn't understand was why the man had ridden away. Now that he was on foot, the job would be easier.

Should be easier.

He reached down and pulled his rifle free, then set off in the direction of the ranch on foot, his rifle in his left hand. He was ready, should the gunman make another move.

He was closer to the ranch than he had thought, and the walk didn't take long. As he approached on foot, several men stopped what they were doing and watched him.

"I'd like to speak to the foreman," he announced, "or the owner."

"What about?" one man asked, stepping forward.

"About buying a horse."

"We ain't got any to sell," the man said. He was tall, broad-shouldered, with red hair and a red mustache.

"Are you the owner?"

"No."

"The foreman?"

"Yeah, I'm the foreman," the man said, "and we ain't got any horses to sell."

Clint looked past the man, into the corral, where there were at least twenty horses, apparently unbroken. In a second corral, two men had obviously been in the process of breaking horses when he arrived.

"You've got quite a few unbroken horses, there," Clint said.

"Mister," the red-haired man said, "maybe you don't hear so good."

"I'd like to see the owner," Clint said, which was a slap in the face to the foreman.

"You're talking to me—" the man began.

"Now I'd like to talk to the owner," Clint said, interrupting him.

"And I say you're finished talking to anybody," the foreman said, taking a step forward.

He was a few inches taller than Clint, and about twenty pounds heavier. On top of that, Clint was weary from the walk. He didn't relish taking the man on in a fight, but he wasn't going to back down, either.

Clint looked around until he caught the eye of another man and then asked him, "Is he always this pleasant?"

"Unpleasant, most of the time," the man said. "Downright mean, other times."

"Hey," the foreman shouted at Clint, "you talk to me, friend, nobody else."

"You and I are finished talking," Clint said. He could see the main house from where he was, and he started in that direction.

"Where do you think you're going?" the foreman demanded.

Clint ignored him.

The foreman waved his arm, and three men barred Clint's path to the main house. The Gunsmith stopped, his rifle resting easily on his shoulder, pointing behind him, and he didn't turn around.

"I asked you a question," the foreman said.

"What's your name?" Clint asked, without turning.

"Meade," the foreman answered, without thinking.

"Mr. Meade," Clint began, "you've been very nasty and unreasonable. I don't want to talk to you anymore, I want to talk to the owner."

"I told you—"

"If these three men in front of me don't move within the next minute, I'm going to put a hole in you with this rifle."

THE PANHANDLE SEARCH

To illustrate his point, the Gunsmith tipped the rifle so that the barrel was pointing directly at the foreman. He aimed from memory, and from the sound of the man's voice, and he was right on target.

Meade laughed nervously and said, "I'll plug you before you can turn around."

Shaking his head Clint said, "I won't have to turn around, Meade. Your men have forty seconds left."

It got very quiet and Meade looked around nervously. The barrel of the rifle was pointing right at him, and the man wasn't even looking at him. How could that be?

"Twenty seconds."

Meade's gunhand was sweating so much he was afraid to go for his gun for fear that it might slip out of his hand.

"Ten seconds."

Meade made an angry, chopping motion with his hand and the three men moved out of Clint's way. When they did, Clint could see that they had been standing between him and a woman, a tall, very handsome woman, who seemed to be amused by what had just transpired.

"Who are you?" he asked.

She smiled at him and said, "I'm the owner."

"Mrs. Press, I'll take care of this—" Meade began, but it was the woman who cut him off.

"I know, Meade," she said. "I can see how well you were handling it." She directed her attention to Clint and asked, "What's your name?"

"Adams," the Gunsmith said, "Clint Adams."

"Well, I'm Beverly Press, Mr. Adams," she said. "You wanted to talk to me, so if you'll follow me to the house, we'll talk."

"Thank you, Mrs. Press."

"Meade," she said, looking at her foreman, "get back to

work. Mr. Adams? This way, please."

She started for the house and Clint followed, aware without looking of the murderous glare he was receiving from Meade.

SIX

Clint followed the woman to the house. She walked with a purposeful, almost masculine confidence, but left no doubt about her femininity. She wore pants which fit rather tight, and Clint enjoyed the sight of her undulating behind as he trailed her.

When they entered the house she brought him into a large, spartanly furnished room, which looked like a man's office. She walked around a large, oak desk and seated herself comfortably. The look on her face was still one of amusement.

"This was my husband's office," she said. "He conducted all of his business from here while he was alive. Now I think he conducts it all from a considerably warmer climate."

"I see."

"Have a seat, Mr. Adams," she said. "Tell me what it is you and my foreman were . . . discussing."

"A horse."

"Just a horse?"

"That's all I wanted," Clint said, "to buy a horse."

"And was my foreman's price too high for you?"

"His attitude was too high for me," Clint said. "He refused to even discuss the possibility of selling me a horse."

"Well, that's odd."

"I thought so."

"Selling you a horse would certainly be in keeping with our business. I can't understand why he would refuse."

"Maybe your foreman is not the businessman you think he is," Clint suggested.

"Businessman?" Beverly Press repeated, laughing. "I don't keep Meade around because he's a good businessman, Mr. Adams. Believe me. Meade has . . . other uses, but his business sense is nonexistent."

"I understand."

"I'm sure you do," she said. "Did you come in on foot?"

"Yes."

"What happened to your horse?"

"The one I was using was shot out from under me on my way here."

"That's an interesting bit of news," she said. "Why do you say the one you were using?"

"There's a story involved—"

"I like stories, Mr. Adams—Clint. I'm very bored out here since my husband died. You can understand that, having met Meade, can't you?"

"Yes."

"Would you like to come upstairs with me, Clint?"

"To tell you the story?"

She smiled and said, "Among other things, yes, to tell me the story . . . and to come into my bed with me." Before he could answer she said, "There's a word I've heard once or twice before, that I've never used myself, but I think it would apply here." She leaned forward, folded her hands and said,

THE PANHANDLE SEARCH

"Clint, would you like to come upstairs and fuck me?"

"That all depends," he answered.

"On what?" she asked, looking surprised.

"On whether or not we can talk about selling me a horse afterward."

She laughed and said, "You're delightful. Yes, of course we can talk about a horse afterward."

"In that case, Mrs. Press," he said, standing up, "I'd love to come upstairs and fuck you."

SEVEN

Once again he followed Beverly Press's impressive backside, this time up the stairs to the second floor, where she proceeded to give him an even better view than he'd previously had.

Undraped, Beverly Press left absolutely no doubt about her femininity. Her breasts were large, firm, tipped with large, dusky nipples. Her waist was trim, with just a hint of the fact that she was forty years old. Her legs were long, smooth and well-muscled.

"*You're* delightful," he said.

"Take off your clothes," she said, and then went to help him do so.

When they were both undressed she led him to the bed and they fell on it together. *The things I have to do to buy a horse,* Clint thought, as he lowered his mouth to her breasts.

If Beverly Press ran her ranch the way she made love, Clint had no doubt that her spread would continue to grow. She was energetic and inventive and insistent, and it was all he could do to keep up with her. Once, when he thought he

THE PANHANDLE SEARCH

wasn't going to be able to do it, he thought of Duke, and he was able to hold back until Beverly was ready.

"Oh, God," she said afterward. Staring down at him she said, "You know you're the first man I've ever been able to find who could keep up with me *and* satisfy me."

He stared up at her and asked, "Does that mean I can buy a horse?"

"You bastard," she said, punching him hard on the chest, "you can *have* a horse, damn you!"

"That's all right," Clint said, reaching for her, "I'll buy one."

Beverly Press walked Clint back to the corral and said, "You can have your pick from anything in the corrals and the barn."

"What price?"

"You'll pay a fair price, Clint," she said. "Can you stay for dinner?"

"I wish I could."

"That must be some horse you're looking to get back," she said. "I wish you luck."

"Thanks."

She called over one of the hands and said, "Mr. Adams will be looking over the horses, looking for one to buy. He's to see everything we have."

"Yes, ma'am."

"If Meade gives you a problem, send him to see me," she instructed the man.

"Yes, ma'am."

With that she turned and walked back to the house without looking back.

"Nice lady," Clint said.

The hand looked at him sideways, then said, "That's what the foreman thinks. Come on, I'll show you the horses."

They went through the horses in the corral, which were unbroken, and Clint decided that he didn't have time to wait for one to be broken. He sure as hell wasn't going to do it himself.

"Let's look in the barn."

The hand led him into the barn, where they went stall by stall until the hand said, "That's it. That's all of them."

"There's another stall," Clint said, pointing to it. The stall in question had been built away from the others, so that it stood alone at the rear of the barn.

"Oh, that's, uh, that was Mr. Press's horse."

"So?"

"So, uh, Meade said nobody's ever to—"

"Mrs. Press said I was to see every horse you've got," Clint reminded him.

"I know, but—"

"Is there a horse in that stall?"

"Ha!" the man said. "There sure as hell is."

The man was obviously impressed with the animal housed within that stall.

"I'd like to see it."

"I don't think Mrs. Press meant—"

"Maybe you better go and ask her," Clint suggested.

"Uh, yeah, maybe I should," the man said, and he hurried from the barn as Clint approached the stall.

The stall was totally enclosed, which was odd, so that Clint would not be able to look at the horse without opening the door.

He opened it, and caught his breath.

"Well, look at you," he said, admiring the animal in the stall.

The horse was nearly Duke's size and, in fact, was nearly Duke's twin, except for the fact that it was white. Clint leaned over far enough to be able to tell that there was another difference. Duke was a gelding.

Clint stepped into the stall and reached for the horse's neck. Although the animal shifted his feet nervously, he did not draw away from the Gunsmith's touch, and soon Clint was stroking the horse with both hands.

"Impressive, isn't he?" Beverly Press asked. Clint turned and saw her standing at the stall door.

"He certainly is," Clint said. "He's almost as impressive as Duke."

"Really?" she asked, looking surprised. "My husband always said that Lancelot was the finest hunk of horseflesh he'd ever seen."

"I'm sure he was right," Clint said.

"I wish I could see that horse of yours," she said.

"I'll bring him back this way," Clint said.

"Sure."

"Lancelot, huh?" Clint said, half to himself, stroking the horse's neck.

"That was a knight in King Arthur's court," Beverly said.

"Yes, I know," Clint said. "How much do you want for him?"

She ran her eyes over the horse and said, "I did say any horse, didn't I?"

"Yes, you did," Clint said, walking to the stall, "but I'll understand if you change your mind. I guess I could take one of the others—"

"No, that's not necessary," she said, touching his arm. "Lance shouldn't be kept cooped up in this stall all the time, anyway."

"You keep him in here all the time?" Clint said incredulously. "What a waste!"

"Not all the time," she said. "I let him out in the corral

from time to time, but the problem is, no one has ever been able to ride him but my husband."

"I see."

"So I guess what I'm saying is," she said, "if you can ride him, you can have him."

Clint looked at Beverly, then at Lancelot, and said, "That sounds fair enough."

As Beverly Press left the stable, Clint moved back into the stall and laid his hand on the big white horse's neck.

"We won't have any trouble getting along, will we, boy?" he asked.

The big horse looked at him and seemed to understand what he was saying. Again Clint was struck by the similarities between the white Lancelot and his own black Duke.

"Come on," Clint said, grabbing a bridle from a nail on the wall of the stall, "let's see if we can't get someone to go out and get my saddle, and then we'll go for a little get-acquainted ride."

Clint led Lancelot outside and found the hand who had originally shown him the horses. The man agreed to send someone out to retrieve the Gunsmith's saddle, and Clint spent the time walking the white horse around the corral, getting to know him a little better.

When two hands finally returned with his saddle and gear, he thought he had the horse won over. Most of the ranch hands, and the foreman, Meade, gathered around the corral to see if indeed he had. He took his time saddling the horse, talking to him the entire time, and by the time he was ready to mount, Beverly Press had joined the crowd around the corral. If they were hoping to see the Gunsmith thrown, or even have trouble with the horse, they were all very disappointed.

Clint mounted up without any difficulty whatsoever, and knew that he and Lancelot understood each other.

"I'll be damned!" Meade snapped as Clint rode Lancelot around the corral, with the horse acting as meek as you please.

"Well," Beverly Press called out to him, "I guess the horse is yours."

Clint rode over to where Beverly was sitting on the fence and said, "For a fair price."

"Take him, or borrow him," Beverly said, "but I won't take your money, Clint."

"Beverly—"

"That's my final offer," she broke in. "Take it or leave it."

Clint patted Lancelot on the neck a few times, then said to Beverly, "If you put it that way, I guess I'll take it. I'll bring him back when I've recovered Duke."

As the ranch hands dispersed, talking among themselves about what they had just seen, Beverly Press asked Clint, "What happens if you don't?"

Shaking his head, the Gunsmith said, "That's just not one of the possibilities I'm considering."

Clint rode his new horse back to town, where he put him up at the livery. Lester recognized the horse but simply raised his eyebrows and kept quiet. By now he had come to realize that Clint Adams was an unusual man.

Clint spent the night in his hotel room, once again saying good-bye to Brenda, then checked out the following morning, left his rig and team in the capable hands of Lester and rode out of Little Creek, Wyoming on the white horse he had decided to call "Lance," and headed for Texas.

EIGHT

At that moment, Moose Chandler was having a meeting with his foreman, Matt Turquette, in his office.

Turquette was a big, beefy man who had worked for Chandler for twelve years, starting out as a hand and working his way up to foreman. On top of being big, he was notorious for being mean, a condition that became worse anytime he heard one of his men call him "Turkey," when they thought he wasn't listening. He responded to the nickname "Turk," but when it came to "Turkey," he had a short fuse. Turk was afraid—and his fear was mixed with respect—of only one man: his boss, Moose Chandler.

"I don't know why I let you hire these misfits," Chandler said loudly. When Moose Chandler spoke loudly, it was like thunder, but Turk still preferred it to when his boss really got mad and started to yell. "A man with one hand, a man with one eye, and now a man with half a brain. What the hell was he thinking of?"

"He said he was trying to scare Adams into not following you," Turk said.

THE PANHANDLE SEARCH 33

"Damn it, Turk, I told you I didn't want to make this trip without you!" Chandler boomed.

"They're good men, Mr. Chandler. Wilson just got carried away."

"I wish he would."

The three men Moose Chandler had taken with him on the business trip that had taken him through Little Creek, Wyoming were Roy Watson, One-Eye Doran and Lefty Barron. Lefty and Watson had braced Clint Adams in the livery, and Doran had hit him from behind. Doran was the one who had been bitten by Duke while they were trying to blindfold him and hobble him, and Watson had stayed behind to take a few shots at Clint to try and scare him.

"Watson better get back here in time to get fired," Chandler said. "If he gets caught by Adams, he can have the law on us. Without Watson, he's got nothing. No proof."

"Roy'll get back, Mr. Chandler," Turk said.

"He'd better. What about those other two idiots?"

"Lefty took One-Eye into town to get that bite looked at again," Turk said.

"Good. Maybe it'll get infected and fall off, then together they'd make one whole, three-eyed man."

"Mr. Chandler, I'm sure Lefty really had no intention of shooting that horse. It was just—"

"I don't care what it was," Chandler said, interrupting loudly. "Keep the man away from my horse, you understand?"

"Yes, sir."

"You handle the horse, Turk. He'll respond to you. You're the best horseman I know."

"I appreciate that, Mr. Chandler," Turk said, "but this is no ordinary horse."

"I know it," Chandler said, and his eyes seemed to glow. "That's why I wanted him in the first place."

"He won't let anyone near him—" Turk began to argue.

"Then it's up to you to change that," Chandler said. "Gentle him. You've done it before."

"With two-year-old wild ones, yes, but not with a six-year-old gelding who is apparently set in his ways."

"What are you trying to tell me, Turk?"

"This is a one-man horse, Mr. Chandler," Turk said, hoping his boss wouldn't react too violently to his opinion. "He'd kill any one of our men rather than let him ride him."

"I'm leaving it up to you to change his ways, Turk," Chandler said. "That's what I'm paying you for."

"Yes, sir."

"And keep those idiots away from him," Chandler said.

"They did get him here, sir, from Wyoming," Turk reminded Chandler, in defense of his men.

"Only with me there to keep them from killing him, and him from killing them."

"Yes, sir," Turk said, again.

"Now, I want you to put a man in town to be on the lookout for Adams. I also want you to check him out and find out who he is."

"Sir?" Turk asked, looking confused.

"Are you deaf, man? I want to know who this fella is. I want to know if I can expect him to come after his horse."

"Well, sir, I'd say you definitely can."

"Why do you say that?"

"Uh, it never occurred to me that you wouldn't know who Clint Adams is."

"Do you mean you know who he is?"

"Yes, sir."

"Then why didn't those idiots know?" Chandler asked. "Never mind. Just tell me who he is so I'll know what to expect."

"He's an ex-lawman they call the Gunsmith, Mr. Chan-

THE PANHANDLE SEARCH

dler," Turk said. "You know that name, don't you?"

Chandler frowned then, and Turk was afraid for a moment that the Moose was going to lose his temper.

"Of course," Chandler said softly, "of course, I know *that* name."

Moose Chandler lapsed into a thoughtful silence, and Turk remained quiet waiting for his boss to sort out his thoughts. Maybe, he thought, the Moose was beginning to realize what he had done.

"Well," Chandler finally said, "what's done is done. I suppose there's no question that Adams will come after his horse."

"No, sir."

"We'll just have to be ready for him," Chandler said. "Make sure you put a good man in town, Turk, and not one of your goddamn misfits."

"Yes, sir."

"All right, get out. Make sure that horse is well cared for, and watched. I don't want him getting away, or hurting himself trying to get away."

"You can count on me, Mr. Chandler," Turk said. He turned and left and Chandler poured himself a drink.

He examined the amber liquid in his fine, crystal glass and then looked around at his plush office, which was his favorite room in the thirteen-room house. Then he thought about the magnificent animal he had stolen from the Gunsmith, and weighed them against each other.

"The goddamn Gunsmith!" he snapped. He knocked back the drink, emptying the glass, then wiped his mouth with his hand and muttered, "Shit!"

NINE

By the time Clint Adams rode into Labyrinth, Texas he was thoroughly impressed with his new mount. The horse's stamina almost rivaled Duke's—though Lance was a couple of years younger and Duke still had the edge.

At the livery the liveryman greeted Clint with a wide smile, and then a frown. "Clint, what the hell happened to Duke?"

Dismounting, Clint said, "I just painted him white, that's all. Got tired of black all the time."

Still frowning, the liveryman moved closer to inspect the white horse, then stepped back shaking his head. "If I didn't know better, I'd swear you was telling the truth. What goes on?"

"I just borrowed this horse, Dan," Clint said, "until I get Duke back."

"Get him back?" the man asked. "What do you mean? Did you lose him?"

"Let's just say he's temporarily misplaced," Clint said,

removing his saddlebags and rifle from his saddle. "Just treat him as you would Duke, Dan, okay?"

"Sure, Clint, sure," the liveryman said, his frown deepening.

Over the past few years, Labyrinth had become sort of an unofficial home base for the Gunsmith, which was odd when you consider that this was the town where he first heard of the death of his good friend, Wild Bill Hickok.* He had made a few friends while in this town, and had taken to stopping in whenever he was in Texas. Soon he was receiving mail there and had opened a bank account. The one thing he had avoided cultivating in Labyrinth was a woman. He did not want to have a woman here, constantly waiting for him to show up, and then crying every time he left.

He went to the hotel, where he was greeted by the clerk, left his gear in his room, and then walked over to the saloon that was owned by a man who had become one of his best friends, Rick Hartman.

"How are you, T.C.?" he said to the tall, slim bartender.

"Better than you, from the looks of you," the bartender replied.

Clint put his hand to his jaw and felt almost a week's growth there.

"Yeah, I guess I need a bath and a shave, all right," he said, "but first a beer."

"You've got it."

When T.C. returned with a mug of chilled beer Clint asked, "Where's the boss?"

"In his office," the barkeep replied.

"Alone?"

T.C. shook his head solemnly and said, "He's interviewing a new girl."

The Gunsmith #14: Deadman's Hand

"Ah."

"A nice one too," the bartender added.

Pushing away from the bar Clint said, "Well, I'm sure he won't mind sharing the wealth."

"You'd know better than I would," T.C. said.

Clint took his beer and walked to the back of the room, where he knocked loudly on the door. When there was no answer, he pounded on the door again. He could hear footsteps approaching the door from the inside, and from the sound of them, Rick was more than slightly angry.

"God damn it—" he said as he swung the door open angrily, but when he saw who it was his anger faded and he said, "I should have known."

"Hello, Rick," Clint said. "Have a drink with me?"

Rick stood there a moment, hair messed, collar open, and then waved past Clint to the bartender and said to Clint, "Come on in. There's someone here you might enjoy meeting."

As Rick backed away, Clint entered and saw the girl. She was a tall brunette, about twenty-three, with opulent curves tucked into a tight, blue sequined dress. She was patting her hair into place, and her mouth needed a fresh coat of lip gloss. Rick was wearing most of the original coat on his own mouth.

"Oh, I'm sorry," Clint said with exaggerated politeness. "Am I interrupting something?"

"Not at all," Rick said, removing a handkerchief from his breast pocket and wiping his mouth. "Clint Adams, I'd like you to meet Cindy Meriweather. I've just hired her."

"Welcome to Rick's, Cindy," Clint said, raising his mug to welcome her.

"Clint is a regular customer," Rick said, seating himself behind his desk. "He shows up about once every six months and bums a beer."

At that point, before the girl even had an opportunity to

THE PANHANDLE SEARCH

speak, T.C. entered the office carrying a second mug of beer for the Gunsmith, and a fresh mug for Rick.

"T.C., Cindy's hired. Take her outside and get her started, all right?"

"Oh, thank you, Rick—" the girl began, but Rick cut her off before she could gush further.

"That's okay, kid," Rick said. "Now get to work while I get reacquainted with my friend, here."

"Sure, Rick, sure," she said.

"Come on, kid," the bartender said. He allowed her to precede him out of the room, and then shut the door behind them.

"Well," Rick said, picking up his beer, "to what do I owe this interruption?"

"Moose Chandler," Clint said.

"What about him?"

"What do you know about him?"

"He's a dangerous man with half of Texas in his pocket," Rick said. "Why?"

"He's got Duke," Clint said, staring into his beer.

Rick leaned forward and said, "What?"

"You heard me," Clint said.

"How the hell did that come about?"

Both men nursed their beers while Clint told his story.

"I think we both need another beer," Rick said. Clint started to get up to get it and Rick said, "Sit tight, I'll get them. You must be tired from your long walk."

"What long walk?"

"From Wyoming to Texas," Rick said on his way to the door with the empty mugs.

Clint laughed as Rick went out; the saloon owner returned moments later with two fresh, cold beers. He set one down on his desk in front of Clint, then walked around and seated himself with the other beer in front of him.

"Chandler's place is like a fortress, Clint," he said, finally. "He's got eyes and ears in half of Texas."

"I'll just have to approach him from the other half, then," Clint said.

"You're too late."

"Why?"

Rick sipped his beer and said, "Because you're already in his half."

"Labyrinth?"

Rick nodded, "We're in Chandler country, pal. He already knows you're here."

TEN

"That's good, then," Clint said, after a moment.

"What do you mean, good?" Rick asked.

"If Chandler knows I'm coming, maybe he'll get nervous," Clint said.

"Are you relying on that reputation you hate so much, all of a sudden?" Rick asked, frowning.

"Rick," Clint said, "I'll rely on anything I have to in order to get Duke back."

Rick paused a moment, then said, "Well, I really can't argue with you there—but Chandler's got an army at his beck and call, Clint, and a good man to lead them for him."

"Who is that?"

"Fella by the name of Turquette—they call him 'Turk,' unless they want to get him mad, in which case they call him 'Turkey,' but nobody in their right mind wants to get him mad."

"Why not?"

"The man is a bull, that's why. He can break an average man in half with his bare hands."

"It looks like I'm going to need my hunting rifle," Clint said. "First a moose, now a bull."

"Don't take it lightly, Clint."

"I'm not, Rick, but they'd better not take me lightly, either."

"I don't think anyone would take the Gunsmith lightly," Rick said. "In fact, they may take you too seriously and try to kill you before you reach Chandler's."

"They've already tried," Clint said, and explained how someone had taken a couple of shots at him while he was shopping for a horse.

"There you go, then," Rick said. "You're going to need some help on this."

"I appreciate the offer, Rick—"

"Hey, I wasn't volunteering," Rick hastened to add. "I know my limitations, Clint, ol' buddy. I run a hell of a saloon and I can handle any trouble that comes along in my place, but beyond that—"

"Sure, Rick," Clint said, remembering that Rick had once pulled his chestnuts out of the fire when he had been too drunk to do it for himself.

"I can probably get you some help, though," Rick said.

"I'll tell you what," Clint said, setting his empty mug down on the desk. "You see who you can round up, and I'll let you know if I need them."

Clint stood up and Rick asked, "How long do you plan on staying in town?"

"Not long," Clint said. "I'm going to rest my horse and stock up on some supplies. I'll probably pull out in the morning."

"You heading for Sweetwater?"

"That's the nearest town to Chandler's spread, isn't it?" Clint asked.

"It is."

THE PANHANDLE SEARCH

"Then that's where I'm heading," Clint said.

"Well, you'd better get a bath first, or they'll not only see you coming, they'll smell you coming."

"Thanks for the advice," Clint said.

As Clint made for the door Rick called out to him.

"Yeah?"

"What I said before—" Rick began, then stopped and tried again. "If you need any help, you give a holler, hear?"

"I hear, Rick," Clint said. "Thanks."

Clint went back to the hotel and got himself a bath and a shave. When he passed the front desk on the way back to his room he noticed that the clerk was grinning at him, as if he knew something the Gunsmith didn't.

"What's on your mind?" Clint asked, stopping at the desk.

"Nothing, Mr. Adams," the young man said, "nothing at all."

"I've been in this hotel before, boy," Clint said, "and you know I don't like surprises."

"Yes, sir," the kid said, nervously.

"Then give."

"She said she was from Rick's, Mr. Adams," the boy said, now openly nervous, "that's the only reason I let her go up, honest. I didn't mean no—"

"Describe her."

The kid did so, with obvious relish, and the description matched the girl Rick had been interviewing when Clint interrupted them.

"It's okay," Clint assured the shaken clerk, "she's from Rick's."

The clerk sighed with relief, and Clint went up the steps to the second floor. As he approached the door to his room he put his right hand on the butt of his gun, which was hanging from his shoulder, in its holster. He didn't know the girl, and obviously Rick didn't know her either. There was no reason for him to think that she was paying him a social call.

He turned the doorknob with his left hand, keeping his right hand on the butt of his gun, and pushed the door inward.

Cindy was sitting in his bed with the sheet about her waist, and her opulent curves were no longer covered by the tightly fitting gown. They were there for all the world to see, and they were impressive.

"Well, hello," he said, stepping inside. He took a quick glance behind the door before closing it.

"Hello, Mr. Adams," she said.

"Would you mind telling me what you're doing here?"

She cupped her full, brown-nippled breasts in her hands and asked, "You mean aside from the obvious?"

"That's what I mean."

"Well, Rick did say that you were a regular customer," she told him, "and the bartender explained that part of my job was to make sure that the regular customers were kept happy."

"And that's what you're doing here?" he asked.

She flicked her thumbs over her distended nipples and asked, "Don't you think I have what it would take to make you happy—even for a while?"

"Did Rick send you up here?" he asked, taking the holster off his shoulder and hanging it on the back of a chair.

She shook her head and said, "It was all my idea. Something passed through me in Rick's office when I saw you," she added. "Didn't you feel it?"

"Frankly," he replied, "no."

She pouted and put her hands out to him. "Why don't you come over here and I'll see if I can't make you feel it?"

She was a beautiful woman, there was no denying that, and

THE PANHANDLE SEARCH 45

there was also no denying the effect she was having on him. The sight of those large breasts and hard nipples had given him a raging erection, which was demanding some attention at the moment. He took the holster from the back of the chair, walked to the bed and hung it on the bedpost, within easy reach.

"You're not going to need that," she said, reaching for him and undoing his pants. "This is all you'll need."

She had his pants open and pulled out his rigid cock, eyes widening as it came into view.

"Oh, yes," she whispered. She put one hand beneath his penis and, leaning forward, guided his pulsating cock into the sweet depths of her mouth. As she began to suck at him avidly, she slid her hand down so that she was cupping his balls gently, almost lovingly.

Clint almost closed his eyes in response to her ministrations, but he retained some semblance of control over his senses and forced himself to keep them open. Moaning, he cupped the back of her head in his hands as she increased the force of her suction. When she felt that he was ready to come, she allowed him to slide free of her mouth.

"Come on," she said, lying back on the bed so that he could see every delectable inch of her. Very deliberately, she slid two fingers into her mouth, sucked on them until they were gleaming, and then she reached down and sunk them into the wetness of her vagina. When she removed them they shone differently now, from her love juices, and she said again, "Come on, Clint Adams. I want you inside of me."

He leaned forward, putting his hands and knees on either side of her. She touched her wet fingers to his lips, and he took both of them into his mouth and licked them clean, savoring the taste of her.

"God," she said, "seeing you do that makes me hot.

Please, Clint, please," she went on, putting her arms around him, "put it in me . . . now!"

As she said "now!" he drove his hardness into her, sliding into her slick passage with incredible ease. He fought to maintain his awareness of his surroundings, but as she slid her powerful legs around him, and used her muscles to suck at him, it became increasingly difficult to think of anything but the eager, willing woman beneath him. Clint had been on the trail for a long time and he reveled in the feel and smell of her.

The Gunsmith, however, remained aware.

"I'm impressed," she said, later.

"So am I," he replied. "What is it that impressed you?"

"I know what impressed you," she said, smiling and running her hand over his chest, "but I'm talking about something else. You were able to satisfy me—boy, were you ever!—but throughout it all, I had the feeling that you would have been able to get to your gun at a moment's notice."

"You're a beautiful, sexy woman, Cindy," Clint said, "but I've found out in the past that beautiful and sexy also go with dangerous."

"Dangerous? Me?" she asked, sitting up.

"What brought you to Rick's?" he asked. "And what brought you up here to me?"

"I have to get back to work," she said, getting out of bed and starting to get dressed. "I don't want to get fired on my first day on the job."

"Who are you, Cindy Meriweather?" Clint asked. "Who sent you? Chandler?"

She slipped into her dress and said, "I don't know anyone by that name. I told you why I came up here."

"Something passed through you when you saw me," he repeated.

THE PANHANDLE SEARCH 47

"That's right," she said, "I had to come up here, and I'm glad I did, even if you aren't."

"Oh, I'm happy with the physical part of it," he said. "You are incredible in bed."

"Thank you," she said. "Would you secure my dress, please?"

He did up the buttons on the back of her dress, and she smoothed it down over her hips and thighs with a thoroughly feminine, sexy gesture.

"Will you be in town long?" she asked.

He almost told her the truth, the question had come so smoothly, but he caught himself and said, "I haven't decided yet."

"Well," she said, pausing at the door, "when you do decide, let me know, huh?"

"Don't worry," he told her, and as she went out the door, closing it behind her he added, "you'll be the first to know."

Clint fell asleep after Cindy Meriweather left, and when he awoke it was early evening. His stomach was telling him that it was time for dinner, and he had a standing invitation to dine with Rick whenever he was in town. He was feeling pretty depressed about having gone so long without yet recovering Duke, and he considered skipping dinner with Rick this time, but he had some new questions to ask him, specifically about Cindy Meriweather.

He'd had women tumble into bed with him at a moment's notice before, but this time it didn't strike him as right. He knew that Rick had hired new girls in the past, but the coincidence of her being hired just as he came to town, and then climbing into bed with him was too much, especially with a man as powerful as Moose Chandler expecting his arrival in Texas. A man with that much power used people as tools, and Cindy Meriweather might just prove to be one of those tools. If she did, then he might be able to turn her to his own advantage.

Whether she wanted to or not.

"You wanted to see me, Mr. Chandler?" Turk asked, presenting himself to Moose Chandler in his office.

Chandler had a map of Texas spread out on his desk, and now he looked up from it to his foreman.

"Yeah, Turk," he said, "I been thinking."

"About what, sir?"

"About who we're dealing with here," Chandler said. "I'm going to want to know as soon as possible when he enters the area."

"I've got a man in town, sir, as you ordered," Turk said.

"I know that," Chandler answered, "but I want you to send a man to each of these towns as well."

Turk walked around the desk to stand next to his boss and looked at the towns he was indicating. Lansdale, Wallman, Tobinville, Labyrinth.

"Each of those towns is a half day's ride from here, Mr. Chandler," Turk pointed out.

Chandler sent a hard look his way and said, "Then you better have them leave right away so they only have to make half the trip in the dark."

"Yes, sir."

Turk circled the desk and started for the door, but Chandler called his name before he could get to it.

"Turk!"

"Yes, sir?" Turk said, turning back to face Chandler.

"You've been with me a long time, haven't you?" Chandler asked.

Turk remained quiet for a moment, puzzled by the question, then said, "Yes, sir, I have. About twelve years, the last

THE PANHANDLE SEARCH

four as your foreman."

"You helped me build this place."

"I suppose that's right, sir."

"Why don't you call me by my first name, then?" Chandler asked. "Why is it always 'sir,' or 'Mr. Chandler'?"

Turk turned his hat in his hands and said, "Before you hired me I spent a lot of time in the army, sir, most of it as a sergeant. It was a way of life I liked, and got kind of used to."

"You see me as your commanding officer, then," Chandler said. "Is that it?"

"Yes, sir."

Chandler paused now, seemingly uncomfortable with what he was about to say.

Finally, he said, "Do you think you could ever see me as a friend?"

Now Turk was really puzzled. He'd never heard such a question from Moose Chandler, and had never seen him look uncertain.

"As a friend?" he asked. "I don't see . . . well, why not, sir," he said, because that was what he thought his boss wanted to hear.

"Good," Chandler said. "From now on, then, you can call me Moose."

"All right . . . Moose . . . sir," Turk said.

Chandler nodded and said, "Get those men on their way, then."

"Right away . . . Moose," Turk said. The name did not roll off his tongue easily. He opened the door, stepped outside, and shut it behind him. Then he leaned against it and let out a breath. He'd never heard of Moose Chandler needing a friend before.

Then again, Moose Chandler—who had certainly faced a

lot in his day—had never had to face a legend like the Gunsmith before.

Moose Chandler probably figured that this time he could use all the friends he could get.

That scared the shit out of Matt Turquette.

ELEVEN

"You want to know about Cindy Meriweather?" Rick asked. "You only saw the girl for two seconds, Clint. Did she make that much of an impression?"

"You'll never know what an impression she made," Clint said.

They were having dinner in Rick's office, and the saloon owner frowned across the table at the Gunsmith.

"What's that supposed to mean?"

"Maybe I'm being a little too suspicious," Clint said, "but she showed up in town looking for a job just before I came riding in. That bothers me."

"Well, if you're looking for references, this job doesn't call for any."

"You don't know anything about her at all?"

"Not a thing," Rick said, then leaned forward and added, "You saw to that by interrupting my interview."

"Sorry about that," Clint said.

At that point the cook came in with dinner, and conversation was suspended so that they could get a good start on a complete roast beef dinner.

"In my honor?" Clint asked.

"Hell, no," Rick said. "I was going to have dinner with the young lady in question before you came barging in."

Clint knew that was a lie. If Rick had planned on dinner with Cindy, he would have said so and Clint would have gone to a café for dinner. They'd done that before.

"You play chess," Rick said.

"So?" Clint asked, not that he'd had all that much opportunity to play in years, except with Rick.

"You figure Chandler's already moving his pawns around," Rick said, "and Cindy's one of them?"

"It's a thought that had crossed my mind," Clint admitted.

"It's a thought I don't particularly like," Rick said, picking up a mug of beer.

"Why not?"

"If she's a pawn, then she's trying to make me one too," he answered. "I don't like that."

"Well, maybe she's not," Clint said. "Anyway, I'll be leaving in the morning. What harm can she do?"

"We might as well keep an eye on her, just the same," Rick said. "I'll have T.C. watch her."

"Fine," Clint said. "I'm sure he's had worse jobs in his life."

"I put out a call to some people," Rick said.

"Who?"

"Handy men with a gun that I know," he answered. "They'll be ready if you need them."

"I hope I won't," Clint said. "I'm not looking to start a war, I'm just looking to get in, and get out with Duke."

"What about a little revenge?"

Clint thought about that a moment.

"Maybe later, Rick." He picked up his beer mug. "My

main concern is to get Duke away from Moose Chandler. That ought to hurt him enough until I can get back to him."

Rick held up his own mug and said, "I'll drink to that."

TWELVE

After dinner Clint took Rick over to the livery stable to show him Lancelot.

"I don't know how you do it," Rick said, circling the massive white horse.

"Do what?"

"Come up with the kind of horseflesh you do," Rick said. "First Duke, the most magnificent horse I've ever seen, and now this one, who comes pretty damned close."

"I do it the same way you come up with the women you do," Clint said. "A keen eye."

"You don't do so bad in that area, yourself," Rick reminded him. Still examining Lancelot—without touching him—Rick asked, "Tell me about Cindy."

"Nothing to tell," Clint said. "She came to my room. That was too convenient."

"So you started thinking maybe Moose Chandler sent her," Rick said.

"It's possible," Clint said, "and it's possible he didn't."

"Let me ask you something," Rick proposed, turning his back to the horse.

"What?"

"Why not let him keep the horse?"

"What?"

"Let him keep the horse," Rick repeated. "Is a horse worth getting killed over?"

"A horse isn't," Clint said, "but Duke is. He's my partner, Rick."

"Okay, okay," Rick said. "I guess I just never got all that attached to a horse." He patted Lancelot absently, without realizing it, and then walked away.

"Well, I never got attached to a town the way you have to this one," Clint countered.

"What can I say?" Rick asked, spreading his arms wide. "I'm making money. Should I leave? Hell, no!"

Since he'd answered his own question, Clint did not offer an answer of his own.

"Be good, big fella," he said to Lance, and then he and Rick left the livery and started back to the saloon.

"Feel like some poker?" Rick asked. "I'm sure there's a game or two going on by now, or I could get up a private one."

"I don't think so," Clint said. "I think I'll turn in. I want to get an early start in the morning."

"You really are worried, aren't you?" Rick said.

"Not worried, exactly," he said. "I know a horseman like Chandler is not going to harm Duke. I'm just getting kind of tired of doing without him."

"The replacement doesn't look too bad."

"Lance is okay," Clint said. "Better than any other horse I've ever seen. But there's only one Duke."

The hotel was on the way to the saloon, so Rick walked with Clint.

"There is something you can do for me," Clint said when they reached there.

"What?"

"Check out the telegraph office for me in the morning," Clint said. "See if anyone's sent a telegram since I arrived, then see if anyone sends one after I leave."

"Where should I get in touch with you?"

"Not Sweetwater," Clint said. He thought a moment, then decided on Lansdale. He hadn't been to Lansdale, Texas in years, not since his involvement with a "wet stock" operation that had been going on there, run by the foremen of two rival ranches, one in Texas, and one in Mexico.* "Send it to Lansdale. I'll stop there before I get to Sweetwater."

"You'll have to bypass Sweetwater to get to Lansdale," Rick said.

"I know that, but I don't want to risk getting a telegram at the Sweetwater telegraph office. Send it to Lansdale."

"All right."

"I'll stop by in the morning before I leave," Clint said, "and wake you up."

"What a pal," Rick said. "Why don't we just say goodbye right here. You can stop in again on your way back, when you've recovered Duke."

Clint put out his hand and said, "It was good to see you again, Rick."

Taking his hand Rick said, "My offer still stands, Clint, any time you want to take me up on it."

The offer was to settle in Labyrinth and buy into Rick's saloon.

"It's always in the back of my mind," Clint assured his friend.

"Good luck," Rick said, "and don't forget me if you need help."

"I won't."

The Gunsmith #7: The Longhorn War

THE PANHANDLE SEARCH 57

Clint watched Rick walk towards the saloon, then went into the hotel and wearily climbed the steps to his room. He half expected to find Cindy there waiting for him, and was just as pleased to find that she wasn't. He climbed into bed and fell asleep almost immediately.

Moose Chandler left his house in the middle of the night and walked over to the big barn behind his home. As he entered he took a storm lantern off a hook next to the door and lit it, bathing the inside of the barn in a soft, yellow light. Holding the lantern at shoulder height he walked to the rear of the barn, where he had his men build a special stall. Inside the stall stood Clint Adams's big black, Arabian gelding that Chandler had taken to calling "Devil."

"Hello, Devil," he said, standing a few feet away from the stall.

The stall was specially enforced to handle kicks from Devil's powerful haunches, but he still didn't plan on getting too close.

The horse had proved on more than one occasion that he was potentially a man-killer. He hoped that Turk—or somebody—would be able to gentle the magnificent animal before he did kill someone, or else he himself would have to put a .45 slug in Devil's brain.

It never occurred to Moose Chandler to simply let the animal go.

THIRTEEN

Lansdale, Texas had changed very little since Clint Adams had been there last. It was still the largest town no one had ever heard of. It depended almost solely on the business it got from Enoch Kennedy's ranch, and Kennedy paid a lot of money to keep Lansdale off the map.

Clint put Lance up at the local livery, and then registered in the hotel. Just this once, he had intentions of breaking his rule of checking in with the local law whenever he entered a town. He did not want to announce his presence this close to Moose Chandler's spread.

He dropped his gear off in his room, then sat for a moment and thought about Laura Kennedy, Enoch's daughter, and Lita Martinez, the daughter of Victor Martinez, whose spread was on the Mexican side of the border.

Laura was almost six feet tall in boot heels, and would be about twenty-six by this time. She had marvelous, lush breasts, and had received much more of an education back East than her father had thought he was paying for.

Lita was dark haired and fiery, more than a match for any man's sexual appetites, or wants.

THE PANHANDLE SEARCH 59

Much as he would have liked to stop in and see both of them, he didn't think he'd have the time. Maybe later, after he recovered Duke.

It was mid-afternoon, and he decided to check the telegraph office, and then have lunch.

There was one telegram waiting for him from Rick, and he took it with him to lunch. He found a small café that hadn't existed last time he was in town.

He ordered his lunch, and then read the telegram. According to Rick a rider had arrived in Labyrinth during Clint's last night there, and had sent a telegram the next morning to Sweetwater, saying that the Gunsmith had been there, and had left that morning. The telegram had been addressed to "Turk".

When the waitress brought his lunch, he tucked the telegram away in his shirt pocket and started eating.

There was no doubt about it, anymore. Moose Chandler knew that he was on his way, and the man would be ready for him. Knowing that, Clint was still determined to ride into Sweetwater alone, because riding in with a crew would only push Chandler into making a move. If he rode in alone, Chandler might hold off and simply keep an eye on him. Once he was there, Clint would decide what moves to make, and how to get Duke back. After he had Duke, then he would worry about paying Moose Chandler back.

After lunch Clint ordered a second pot of coffee and finished it at a leisurely pace. He tried to decide whether to make the half day ride to Sweetwater now, or wait until morning. If he started out now, he'd get there after dark. There would be a certain advantage to that, but so would there be an advantage to riding into town in broad daylight.

He doubted that Moose Chandler would know the first thing about psychology—not that he knew all that much, himself. He knew enough, though, to know that riding into

Sweetwater in broad daylight, alone, would throw Chandler off balance and make him think before he moved.

So it was decided. He'd wait until morning and then head for Sweetwater. That left the rest of the afternoon and the evening to kill. He could spend the time sleeping, or playing poker.

Or he could go looking for Laura Kennedy or Estrelita Martinez. He opted for poker.

When he got to the saloon he stepped just inside and stopped. He ran his eyes over the front of the bar, and there they were, three little holes in the front of the wooden bar. He'd put those three holes there, and killed the man who had been standing behind the bar. Beneath those three holes there had been a gaping hole, made by a shotgun blast, but that one had been repaired. That blast had been fired at him, and it had been one of the luckiest moments of his life when it missed.*

He shook thoughts of the past from his mind, walked to the bar and ordered a beer.

Beer in hand he turned his back to the bar to inspect the room, and saw that there were two poker games going, with empty chairs at each table.

A lot of trouble can be avoided, he remembered, by picking the right table.

He watched for a while, and then made his choice. As it turned out, he avoided trouble, but his luck was bad and the only other man at the table with any playing ability cleaned up.

"That's it for me," he said, standing up later that night.

"Come back anytime," said the man with most of *his* money in front of him.

"Thanks."

---

*The Gunsmith #7: The Longhorn War

THE PANHANDLE SEARCH 61

He was undressing for bed when there was a knock on the door. He answered it with his boots and shirt off, clad in pants, only.

"Shucks," she said, "I thought I'd catch you naked."

"Laura Kennedy!" he said, confused, but also glad to see her.

"Hello, Clint," she said. "Can I come in?"

"Of course," he said, shaking his head to dispel the shock of seeing her. He backed up and allowed her to enter, then closed the door.

She'd changed, and all for the better. Her hair was still long, still reddish-brown. Her body was the same also, full and firm. Physically she was the same, but her manner, her demeanor had changed. She carried herself differently, with more confidence.

"Clint," she said, and moved into his arms.

They kissed, and then he held her to him while she kissed his chest, and licked his nipples until they were hard.

Feverishly, her hands fell to his pants and began to undo them, and he went to work on her clothes at the same time.

Her breasts were as marvelously full and firm as they had been the last time they'd been together. He lowered her to the bed and began to suck her nipples into hard little nuggets.

"Oh, yes," she said, cradling his head in her hands, and then taking two handfuls of hair to hold him there.

After a few moments she began to butt her hipbones against his, lifting them off the bed, and she whispered, "God, now, I want it now, Clint!"

As he pierced her to her core her hands were on him, clutching his buttocks, scratching his back, just as he remembered her. Her mouth was alive on his face, and when he felt her belly begin to tremble he allowed himself to come with her, filling her with his milky seed.

When he pulled himself free of her she wasted no time in

reminding him of how talented she was. She wiggled down so that she could clean him off with her tongue, then took him into her mouth and suckled him back to life, again. When he was good and hard again she climbed aboard him, impaled herself, and rode him hard. He reached up to cup her breasts and thumb her large, brown nipples while she closed her eyes and lost herself in the sensations. When he felt her insides clutch at him spasmodically he raised his hips off the bed and she sucked his orgasm from him this time.

Later she lay within the circle of his arms and said, "Oh, how I've missed you, Clint Adams."

"I'm flattered," he said. "I thought by now you'd be married and supplying old Enoch with some grandchildren."

"No," she said into his chest, "I'm not married . . . and my father is gone."

"Gone?"

"He died last year."

"I'm sorry," he said, hugging her. "Who's been running the ranch?"

"I have."

"You?"

She lifted her head and looked at him boldly and said, "And I've been doing a damned good job of it, too."

"I'll bet you have," he said. "You've changed."

"How?" she asked, curiously.

"You're more mature," he said, "and more confident."

"In this?" she asked, fondling him.

"You always had confidence in this," he said, "but now I think you've got confidence in everything."

"You're right," she said, "but sometimes . . ."

"Sometimes what?" he asked.

"Sometimes I wish I had someone . . . to share it with, to talk to, because every once in a while the confidence goes away, and I'm scared, like a little girl."

She put her head down on his chest again and said, "And I don't have anyplace to hide, Clint, like I did when I was a little girl and something scared me. No place to hide at all."

Neither have I, he wanted to tell her. *Neither have I.*

FOURTEEN

"How long are you staying?" Laura asked in the morning. "We were a little too busy last night for me to ask you that."

"I'm leaving this morning," he said.

"Oh."

She lowered her eyes and finished buttoning her blouse. "We didn't get a chance to talk. No chance that you could . . . stay awhile longer."

"No," he said, "not much further than, say, breakfast."

She looked up at him and smiled.

"I'll buy it," she said.

Over breakfast he told her exactly why he had come to Lansdale again.

"I guess it was too much to hope for—" she started to say, but she caught herself and stopped. "Still got Duke, huh?"

"I will when I get him back."

"You will," she said. "I have confidence in you."

"Thanks."

"Clint."

"Yes?"

THE PANHANDLE SEARCH 65

"If you need help, I may have almost as many men as Chandler does—"

"I doubt that," he said, "but thanks, honey."

"Be careful of Chandler, Clint," she said. "My father built up a big spread, but Chandler's is massive."

"Have you ever done business with him, Laura?"

"Of course," she said. "We couldn't be in business in Texas without dealing with Chandler at one time or another. He did a lot of business with my father, but I haven't had too many dealings with him since father died."

"But he knows who you are?"

"I'm sure he does. Why?"

"I'm getting an idea that just might work," he said. "But meanwhile let's get some more coffee."

They ordered a second pot and when it came Laura poured.

"Tell me how you ever knew I was in town," Clint said.

"That's easy," she said. "I saw you when you went into the saloon. I was in town on business."

"Why didn't you come into the saloon?"

"I told you, silly," she said. "I wanted to try and catch you with your pants off."

"You caught me with everything but," he said, "but we took care of that, didn't we?"

"We sure did," she said, dreamily. "Do you think you'll come back this way, after you get Duke back?"

If he had a dime for every woman who asked him if he'd be back . . .

"I can't promise anything, Laura—"

"I know that," she said, quickly, looking embarrassed. "I'm just making conversation so you can form your idea."

"Uh-huh," he said. "Well, you did a good job, because I think I've just about got it pinned down."

"Do you want to tell me about it?"

"I have to," he said, leaning forward, "because you and I are going to do a little business together."

After Clint explained his idea and Laura agreed to go along with it they asked for a pen and paper. Clint finished his last cup of coffee while she filled the paper with writing and signed it, and then she walked him to the livery. When she saw Lancelot, her eyes widened admiringly.

"If I didn't know any better—" she began.

"—you'd swear I'd whitewashed Duke," Clint finished.

"Exactly."

When Lancelot was saddled she walked around him, admiring his lines.

"I know you'd never sell Duke," she said, "but what are you going to do with this one when you get him back?"

"Return him to his rightful owner," Clint said, patting Lance's neck. "I borrowed him."

"Would the owner be willing to sell, do you think?"

"You'd have to take that up with her," Clint said, but he didn't tell her where to find Beverly Press and Laura didn't ask.

Maybe they both thought that would be a reason for him to come back.

FIFTEEN

Clint made good time, thanks to the stamina of the white horse. It was early evening when he rode into Sweetwater, and there were plenty of people still in the streets to witness his arrival.

He allowed Lance to slow to a leisurely stroll, and then stopped to ask someone where the livery was. By the time he'd made arrangements to put Lance up, he was sure he had been seen by enough people for it to get back to Moose Chandler.

Carrying his gear, Clint started in search of a hotel, and on the way he came across the sheriff's office. He decided to go inside and check in.

"Can I help you?" the sheriff asked as he entered. The lawman was a well-fed man in his early fifties who made no effort to rise from behind his desk.

"Good evening, Sheriff," Clint said, approaching the man's desk. "My name is Clint Adams."

"What can I do for you, Mr. Adams?"

"Well, I've just arrived in town and thought I would check

in with you. I imagine you like to keep tabs on strangers."

"Oh, sure," the man said, but he seemed puzzled, "sure I do. Are you, uh, planning on staying in town long?"

"That depends."

"On what?"

"On how long it takes me to complete my business."

"You're here on business, then?"

"That's right," Clint said. This was the one time he had wanted a lawman to react to his name, and this one hadn't. Clint couldn't quite bring himself to say "I'm the Gunsmith" to the sheriff, himself.

"With anyone in particular?" the sheriff asked.

"Moose Chandler."

That made the sheriff's eyebrows rise. "You a friend of Mr. Chandler?"

"No," Clint said, "I've just got some business to conduct with him."

"I see."

The sheriff was still puzzled as to why this man had come into his office in the first place, but at least now he knew that he had to get a message to Moose Chandler that the fella was looking for him. That was part of the job.

"Can you tell what the best hotel in town is?" Clint asked.

"Uh, sure, we only got two. Try Sweethouse."

"You're kidding."

"Why would I?" the sheriff asked seriously.

"Never mind," Clint said. "I'll try Sweethouse. Thanks for the information, Sheriff . . ."

"Beaird."

"Sheriff Beaird," Clint said. "Thanks. Have a nice evening."

"Yeah—" the sheriff began, but Clint turned and walked out on him before he could go any further. If Moose Chandler had the power he was reputed to have, Clint was sure he'd be getting a hurry-up message from Sheriff Beaird very shortly.

As Turk hurried into Moose Chandler's office it occurred to him that he had rarely seen Chandler out of his office since this whole business began. What the hell had possessed him to steal the Gunsmith's horse in the first place? Sure, he was a magnificent animal, but he was a gelding, for Christ's sake. He wasn't even good for breeding purposes. As a horseman, Turk appreciated a beautiful animal, but no animal was worth the risk of going against the Gunsmith.

"What the hell are you barging in here for?" Moose Chandler demanded testily. From the way he looked, he might have been dozing at his desk.

"He's here," Turk said.

"Adams?"

"In town," Turk said. "Rode in bold as you please."

"Alone?"

"Yup."

"Is he crazy?"

"I don't know."

"Did he talk to anyone?"

"Yeah. He talked to Sheriff Beaird."

"That idiot?"

"Beaird was going to send someone out here to tell us, but then he spotted our man in town and told him."

"Told him what?"

"Adams told the sheriff he was here because he had some business with you."

"Is that what he calls it?"

"What do you want to do?"

"For now, nothing," Chandler said, his face looking drawn and tired. "He's alone, what can he do? I think maybe we'll just watch him for a while. Send a man into town to do that—a good man."

"All right."

"And make sure Watson, Doran and Barron stay out of sight," he added. "I don't want Adams to see them."

"I'll keep them busy," Turk promised.

"Yeah, you do that."

Turk turned to leave and Chandler called out, "Turk!"

"What?"

"What's happening with the horse?"

"No luck. Anybody goes near him he goes wild." Turk laughed and said, "He might as well be wild, for all the luck we've been having with him."

"We'll have to try harder."

"What else can we—"

"We'll discuss it tomorrow," Chandler said. "Get a man on his way to town. I want to know every move Clint Adams makes."

"Yes, sir," Turk said, wearily. He was starting to think that it would make better sense to either let the horse go, or just kill him.

SIXTEEN

Clint ate dinner in the Sweethouse dining room, and found that if the name was ridiculous at least the food was good.

And the service.

Clint's waitress was in her late twenties and seemed to be paying special attention to him. She was pretty, if a little harried looking at the moment, and brought him a second pot of coffee just as he was finishing his first.

"How was the dinner?" she asked.

"It was very good," he said.

"And the coffee?"

"Strong, the way I like it."

"Good," she said, seeming relieved. "I'm glad."

"The service was excellent, too," he added. "⟨...⟩uest of the hotel allowed to ask your name?"

"Sure," she said. "My name is Gail."

She was blonde, with a very pretty face⟨...⟩ a nice personality. She was a little on ⟨...⟩ that probably wouldn't have kept her ⟨...⟩ under different circumstances.

71

"I'm Clint," he said.

"Glad to meet you."

"And I'm happy to meet you," he said. "I'll finish this coffee up and you go and see if you can get me a check, all right?"

"Oh," she said, as if he had reminded her of something she'd forgotten, "a check. Sure, right away. I'll get you your check," she said, backing away. She wasn't looking where she was going and bumped into the man seated behind her. Apologizing she turned and hurried away, embarrassed, and Clint laughed.

Sweetwater was the kind of town Lansdale could have been had Enoch Kennedy allowed it. No doubt the town depended heavily on Moose Chandler's ranch, but it would not dry up and die if the ranch should disappear.

The dining room was almost full, and more guests were turning out for dinner, so Clint poured himself another cup of coffee from the second pot, seeking to finish it and leave so someone else could sit down.

He was almost done by the time Gail returned with his check.

"Here it is," she said, handing it to him.

"Thanks," he said. "It seems to be getting busier here, so I think I'll leave, so someone else can use the table."

"All right," she said.

He counted out the amount on the check from his pocket, and then added some for Gail.

"Oh, thank you," she said.

"That's all right," he told her. "Service like yours should be appreciated."

He started to walk away and she said, "Ah, will you be in town long?"

He turned back and said, "I'm not sure. I have some business to transact, and it depends on how long that takes."

"I see," she said. "Well, I guess you'll be eating here again, then."

"I guess so," he said. "Good night, Gail, and thanks again."

"Good night, Clint."

He left, shaking his head and feeling more amused than he had in some time. Gail was refreshing and at a different time he might have pursued her obvious interest in him. He had other things on his mind, however.

Like spotting whoever was watching him.

Chandler would want to be aware of every move he made, especially if he should make a move in the direction of the ranch.

As he left the hotel and crossed the street, he was careful to look unobtrusively in all directions. If someone was watching him, they were not being conspicuous about it. Maybe Chandler hadn't had time to set it up yet.

Clint walked over to one of Sweetwater's saloons, went inside and ordered a beer. It was a small place, but it seemed to be doing a lot of business. There were no gaming tables, but there were a few poker games going on, and all of the tables were full. He figured the odds were pretty good that if a chair opened up and he sat down, he would end up playing against at least one man from Chandler's ranch.

He turned his back and lingered over his beer while keeping an eye on the room through the mirror behind the bar. All right, he was here, in Chandler's bailiwick, and he was sure that Duke was no farther from where he was standing than Chandler's ranch. What he would have liked to do was ride right out there and get him, but that would have been a way to get killed.

He was going to get Duke out, all right. It little longer than he would have liked.

SEVENTEEN

The next morning Clint had breakfast in the dining room, and once again Gail's service was excellent. It was clear that she fancied Clint, but he tried to turn aside her attentions without seeming to be too obvious about it.

After breakfast he decided to take a walk around Sweetwater, with a special eye out for either of the men he had seen in the livery stable at Willow Creek. A one-armed man would be hard put to go unnoticed—unless he was deliberately trying to stay out of sight.

The more he thought about it, the more sense it made that Chandler would keep those two men—and probably the third one, as well, since there was no way they could be sure he hadn't seen him—out of sight. There was only one other of Chandler's men Clint knew anything about, and that was Matt Turquette. All he had to do was have someone point Turquette out to him, and he could take it from there. The letter he carried in his pocket gave him a legitimate reason for king to the foreman of Chandler's ranch, and then to
   himself.

THE PANHANDLE SEARCH 75

On his return trip through town, Clint thought that he had finally picked up the man who was tailing him. He looked bored about the entire thing—on top of looking his age, which was about twenty-one, or so. Clint didn't have the heart to turn around and confront the young man—not yet, anyway. For the moment, he was content to let the fellow follow him to his heart's content.

As he headed back to the hotel, Sheriff Beaird suddenly appeared in front of him, trying his best to look official. He was hindered by the fact that he had to keep hitching his pants up over his ample stomach.

"Can I help you, Sheriff?" he asked.

"I want to talk to you, Adams," the sheriff said.

"Talk away."

"Mr. Chandler is the most respected member of this community," the lawman went on, "and I won't have you harassing him in any way."

"I haven't even seen the man yet, Sheriff. How could I have harassed him?"

"Well," Beaird said, momentarily thrown off balance, "if you had any intentions of harassing him, forget it."

"Sheriff," Clint said, "I told you I had business to transact with Moose Chandler. I'd hardly call that harassment."

"Mr. Chandler don't know you, Adams."

"Well then, maybe you could arrange an introduction," Clint said. "It doesn't have to be Chandler himself. You could introduce me to his foreman, for starters."

"Turk?" the sheriff said. "Adams, you don't want to mess with Turk, believe me."

"You've got me wrong again, Sheriff," Clint said. "If I have business with Chandler, it only makes sense for me to talk turkey with Turk."

The humor of the remark completely escaped the sheriff.

"Look, mister, I'm just warning you for your own good.

Don't mess with Chandler, or Turk. If you want to, you ain't getting me in the middle."

"I wouldn't dream of doing what Moose Chandler has already done," Clint said. He started to walk away and then said, "Oh, and Sheriff, if that stomach gets any bigger, you're going to have to start buckling your belt underneath it, down around your hips. A lawman's got to move fast sometimes. Have a nice day."

Chandler's tail was so close to them, trying to hear what was being said, that Clint couldn't resist looking his way and saying aloud, "Come on, kid. You don't want to get lost."

EIGHTEEN

Clint spent the remainder of the morning in his hotel room, cleaning his guns, and when lunchtime came he got an idea. He went downstairs to the front of the hotel, looking for the boy who was keeping an eye on him. He spotted him, hurriedly ducking into an alley next to the hotel, to avoid being seen. Clint walked over to the mouth of the alley and peered in.

"Hi there," he said to the young man who was flattened against the side of the building. He did everything but close his eyes in an attempt to become invisible.

"What's your name?" Clint asked.

The lad looked at Clint, thought the question over, and finally decided to answer. "My name's Jed Crandall . . . sir."

"You hungry, Jed?"

"Sir?"

"You probably don't have time to eat if you have to stay out here and wait for me to come out so you can follow me. Why don't you come inside and have lunch with me?"

The boy seemed confused by the offer.

"You're supposed to be keeping an eye on me, right?"

"Uh, right."

"Well, what better way to do that than to sit at the same table with me?"

He still looked confused, but he couldn't exactly argue with that, so he said, "A-all right."

"Come on," Clint said. "Lunch is on me and you can have anything you want."

Warily, the boy came out of the alley and followed Clint into the hotel.

Gail rushed over to find out what Clint wanted and took both his and Jed's order.

"When are you supposed to report back to Mr. Chandler?" Clint asked.

"I ain't," Jed said. "I'm supposed to wait until one of the other boys comes to relieve me, and then I report to Turk."

"Why'd they pick you for this job?"

"I guess they thought you wouldn't suspect me 'cause I'm so young," the kid said. "I guess they was wrong."

"I guess so."

"Mister . . ."

"Yeah?"

Jed leaned forward and asked in a hushed voice, "Are you really the Gunsmith?"

"That's what they call me," Clint admitted.

"Gee!" the kid said, with big saucer eyes.

"Does that impress you?" Clint asked.

"I heard all about you!" the kid said. "No wonder the old man is so afraid of you."

"Who said he's afraid?" Clint asked, with interest.

"Nobody said it, exactly," Jed said, "but why else would he want you watched?"

THE PANHANDLE SEARCH 79

"You don't know?" Clint asked.

"Know what?"

"About my business with Chandler?"

Shaking his head the kid said, "All I know is that he wanted you watched close."

Gail came with their orders and while she arranged the table, Clint examined his lunch guest more closely. He had a mop of red hair, and a mass of freckles all over his face. He was tall and bone thin, and judging from what he had ordered for lunch, Clint wondered how he stayed so thin. Maybe he only ordered that much when he wasn't paying.

"You get your orders from Turk, right?"

"That's right," Jed said around a mouthful of food.

"I want to meet Turk, Jed, and I want you to arrange it," Clint said.

"What?" the boy asked, almost choking.

"I have business with Chandler, and I think it's only proper that I start with his foreman."

"You want to take on Turk?"

"I want to *talk* to Turk," Clint answered, "and that's all. You give him that message for me when you're relieved."

"I'll tell him," the boy promised. He stared down at his lunch and Clint said, "Go ahead and finish your lunch, Jed."

"Yes, sir," Jed said, and attacked his food like it was his last meal.

Addressing himself to his own lunch, Clint took a great deal of satisfaction in the fact that it was going to be Matt Turquette, Chandler's foreman, who would take him out to the Chandler ranch.

After lunch Jed said that he thought he ought to go back outside, in case his relief came looking for him.

"It wouldn't do for them to find you in here with me,"

Clint asked, "would it?"

"No, sir," Jed agreed, "I guess it wouldn't."

"In that case," he suggested, "we'll just keep this lunch a secret—"

"Thanks—"

"—until you talk to Turk."

"Turk?" Jed said, and it was easy for Clint to see how much the kid feared Chandler's foreman.

"Turk will kill me," Jed said, looking sick.

"No, he won't," Clint said. "It's not your fault that I spotted you, and I'll tell him that."

"You will?" Jed asked, hopefully.

"Sure," Clint said, "as soon as you give him my message."

"Uh, sure, I'll give him the message," Jed said. Looking puzzled, he stood up and appeared ready to leave, but he finally gave into his curiosity.

"Mr. Adams," he asked, "if you're here to do business with Mr. Chandler, why is he so worried about what you're doing?"

"Jed, have you seen a big black horse at the ranch, brought there within the past two weeks or so?"

"A big black—yeah, I have heard some of the boys talking, but I haven't seen the horse myself. Why?"

"It's my horse," Clint said.

"I don't understand."

"It's simple," Clint said. "Moose Chandler stole my horse, and I'm here to get him back."

"But . . . why would a man like Mr. Chandler have to steal a horse?"

"That's a good question, son," Clint said. "I'll ask him when I see him—but for now, that's our little secret, too." He pinned the boy's ears back with a hard stare and said, "Understand?"

THE PANHANDLE SEARCH

The boy swallowed hard, nodded his head in short jerky motions, and then hurried from the room.

Clint wondered who the boy would fear more now—Matt Turquette . . . or the Gunsmith?

NINETEEN

Clint was in the saloon when Matt Turquette found him.

He knew Turk almost as soon as he entered through the batwing doors, which flew back with almost enough force to knock them off their hinges. Turquette was an impressive sight, a massive man who filled the frame of the doorway, and quieted all the voices in the room simply by appearing.

Clint was seated at a back table with a beer, and watched as the man approached him. He had either seen the Gunsmith before, or someone had described Clint to him very well.

"Adams?" the man said, planting himself squarely in front of Clint. He had legs like tree trunks, and Clint could see the muscles of his arms straining against the fabric of his shirt.

"I'm Adams. What can I do for you?"

"I understand from one of my men that you want to talk to me," Turk said.

"That's right," Clint said. "Have a seat and I'll buy you a beer."

Turk hesitated, then pulled a chair out and sat down. The

THE PANHANDLE SEARCH 83

bartender hurried over with a beer, flicked nervous eyes over both men, and retreated to the relative safety of his bar.

Turk took a healthy swallow of his beer and said, "What can I do for you, Adams?"

"You're Matt Turquette," Clint asked, "foreman for Moose Chandler?"

"I'm Turquette," the man answered, "foreman of the XC Ranch. John Chandler is my boss."

"The way I hear it, 'Moose' fits him a lot better," Clint said.

"Did you ask me here so we could talk about my boss's name?" Turk demanded.

"No," Clint replied, "I asked you to come here because I want you to take me to your boss. I figure that's the only way for me to get there without getting killed."

"What makes you think you'd get killed trying to get to him yourself?" Turk asked.

Clint shrugged. "I have a reputation. I come to town saying that I have business with the biggest man in the county—"

"Try the state."

"All right," Clint said, conceding the point, "the state. What would this man think when he heard that?"

"Do you think Mr. Chandler would be afraid of you?"

"I'm not saying that," Clint said. "All I'm saying is that I stayed alive this long by being a careful man. I intend to stay alive a lot longer."

"What kind of business do you have with Mr. Chandler?"

"I'll tell that to Chandler." Turk leaned forward, looking mean and powerful. Clint was sure that he was both. "All right. You're his foreman."

"That's right."

Clint had expected Turk to react just the way he did, so he

was prepared. He took the letter from his pocket and handed it to Turk.

"What's this?" Turk asked, taking it.

"Read it," Clint said, and for a moment he was afraid Turk might not know how to read, but then the man looked at the paper and began to digest the contents.

"Business," Clint said when Turk had finished. He put out his hand and said, "That's how Mr. Chandler makes his money, isn't it?"

"Yes, it is," Turk said, handing the letter back.

Turk lapsed into silence and Clint could guess what was going on in his mind. Was Clint on the level? The letter was proof that he was acting on behalf of the Kennedy spread, which encompassed a large portion of southern Texas. Not as large as Chandler's spread, but respectable—and they had done business before.

Turk was trying to decide whether he should go ahead and make a decision on his own, or put it off until he could speak to Moose. If he put it off, however, it meant he had doubts, and why would Chandler have doubts about doing this kind of business with the Kennedy ranch?

Did he have something to hide? He couldn't allow the Gunsmith to think that.

"I'll take you to see Mr. Chandler tomorrow," Turk said. He finished his beer, and then stood up.

"Why not now?"

Towering above the seated Gunsmith Turk said, "Because we go when I say so."

Clint shrugged, put the letter back in his pocket, and said, "You're the foreman."

TWENTY

"You told him *what*?" Moose Chandler bellowed.

"I had to, Moose," Turk said.

"Do you think there's a chance that he doesn't know it was my men who took his horse?" Chandler asked.

"It's possible."

Chandler stood stock-still behind his desk, staring at his foreman, and then said, "I guess it is possible."

"The letter is genuine," Turk said. "We've dealt with the Kennedy spread before, with both Enoch and his daughter, Laura."

"I know."

"It would look suspicious for us to turn him down."

"I know that, too!" Chandler snapped. "Let me think a minute. Pour yourself a drink, Turk."

Turk poured himself some of Chandler's fine brandy, even though he knew it was too rich for his blood. He preferred plain whiskey.

"We'd have to get the horse off the grounds," Chandler finally said.

"If we could do it without the devil killing any of our men," Turk said. "Moose, why don't we just open the doors of the barn and the stall and let him go?"

"I want that horse!" Chandler said. "Do you know that that horse is the first thing I ever stole? I mean, ever *really* stole," Chandler said. "Oh, I've outfoxed a few people in business, bending a few rules along the way, but I never really stole anything. Do you think I made that decision lightly?"

"No, not lightly," Turk said, placing the palms of his hands flat on his boss's desktop, "but I think you might have made it a little too quickly."

Chandler stared hard at Turk and said, "Are you questioning a decision of mine?"

Turk had found, over the past few days, that his fear of Moose Chandler had lessened. Maybe it was because Chandler had been looking more and more like just another human being, of late, just another man. He still respected the man, but he hoped that wouldn't fade, as well.

"I get it," Turk said, in a tone he never would have used on Chandler in the past. "I get to call you Moose and be your friend only when I agree with you."

They stared at each other for a few seconds and then to Turk's surprise, Moose looked away first. "All right," he said, "all right. Maybe I made a rash decision, but I'm standing by it. Are you standing with me?"

"You know I'm with you, Moose," Turk said. "As long as you're paying me to be your foreman, I'm with you."

"Then before you bring Adams out here tomorrow to transact his business, you get that horse off the grounds."

"And take him where?"

"I don't know—" Chandler began, but then he stopped himself short as something occurred to him.

"What?" Turk asked.

"That box canyon we used on those strays last year, remember?" Chandler asked. "That would hold him."

"Sure, it'll hold him," Turk agreed, "but the trick is getting him there."

"Well, if it's a trick," Chandler said, "you'd better damn well figure out a way to do it."

TWENTY-ONE

Gail had large, pendulous breasts tipped with big, pink nipples, wide hips and meaty thighs, and Clint was resting on the cushion of her breasts and thighs as he drove himself deeper and deeper inside of her.

She had been waiting for him outside his hotel when he returned from his meeting in the saloon with Turk, and had boldly stated that she wanted to go to bed with him.

"I know I'm not especially beautiful," she had told him, "but my poppa always taught me that you never get nothing unless you ask for it."

He decided to show her just how smart her father really was.

They went to his room and he undressed her, kissing her neck, her breasts, her belly.

"I'm too fat," she gasped as his tongue probed into the silky triangle of fine, blond hair between her legs.

"Shh," he told her, pushing her down on the bed.

THE PANHANDLE SEARCH 89

While he undressed she waited impatiently for him, and when he came to her she held him tightly, so that he couldn't change his mind.

She was by no means fat. Her breasts and thighs were meaty, but firm. He eased out of her grip, spread those thighs and once again began probing with his tongue. She was slick and tasty, and he lapped up as much as he could and then turned his attention to her stiff love button. He flicked at it with his tongue, held it between his teeth and sucked on it, while she beat her fists on his shoulders, and then when she started to come she dug her fingernails into him and lifted her hips off the bed.

"Oh, Jesus—" she moaned, but he gave her no time to catch her breath. His stiff cock was aching too much for him to wait.

He found it odd how excited he was by this girl. He moved up so that he was suspended above her with one hand on each side of her, and then he eased into her inch by steaming hot inch, until the full length of him was firmly inside her.

"Oh God, oh God, oh God," she moaned, as if praying, while he drove himself into her, enjoying the cushion of her ample breasts and thighs. He reached beneath her to cup the firm globes of her butt and began to control their tempo.

"Oh yes, yes, yes . . ." she hissed into his ear as he continued to plow into her mercilessly. "Oh, that's it, just like that, don't stop . . ."

He had no intention of stopping, not until he had satisfied himself. For once he felt like being selfish, and since she didn't seem to be complaining, he continued to work her at his pace, his tempo, until finally he exploded inside of her. He felt his seed spewing out of him in powerful spurts, and felt as if it would never let up. Gail had become a mindless thing beneath him, bucking and moaning and pleading for more, and he went on shooting inside of her until it became almost painful. . . .

Afterward she said, "Do you think I'm bold?"

"Yes."

"Shameless?"

"Yes."

"Terrible."

"No," Clint said, "as a matter of fact, you were quite good."

"You were wonderful," she said.

"Thank you."

She had her head on his right shoulder, and his right arm was curled around so that he could roll the nipple of her right breast between his fingers.

"So you're bold and shameless," he said. "Those are traits I admire and appreciate in a woman, very much."

"I'm glad," she said. "I am overweight, though."

"You'd know I was lying if I argued with you," he said, "but a man once told me that it isn't how much you've got, but how you used it." He cupped her breast in his hand and said, "You used it very well."

"I don't do this often, you know," she said.

"I could tell that."

"Oh? How?" she asked. "Did it show? Was I inexperienced? Was I—"

"You were like a man coming out of the desert who's been led to water," he said, interrupting her.

"Oh," she said, looking sheepish. "Did I want it that badly?"

"Yes," he said, kissing her forehead, "but then so did I."

"Do you know what?" she asked.

"What?"

She reached beneath the sheet to roll him in her fingers and

THE PANHANDLE SEARCH

said, "I want it again."

"What a coincidence," he said. "So do I."

"Hold him!"

"We're trying to!"

"Get the blindfold on him," Turk shouted. "Hobble him!"

"Which do you want first?" asked the man holding the blindfold and the hobbles.

"Do something," one of the two men with ropes on the big black shouted.

They had decided to move Devil during the night, so that Turk could go for Clint Adams early, but it was proving even more difficult than they had thought.

"Get that blindfold on him and he'll calm down," Turk shouted.

The man with the blindfold hesitated, because in order to try and get it on the horse, he'd have to enter the stall. That would put him within reach of those thrashing hooves and gnashing teeth.

"Get it on him, Sykes!" Turk shouted. "Or go and tell Moose why you didn't."

That got the man named Sykes moving. He opened the door to the special stall, went inside, realized that he had not shut the door behind him, and that was the last thing he remembered. As he turned to shut the door, Devil lashed out with his front hooves, and caught the man on the back of the head with one. The blow was not fatal, but it did split Sykes's scalp, causing a lot of blood. As Sykes stumbled out of the stall, the horse took off after him. The two men holding ropes on the big black felt the burning in their hands and released the ropes.

"No!" Turk shouted, but it was too late. He had just

enough time to leap out of the way to avoid being trampled as the horse rushed out of the stable into the night.

"He's gone," Turk told Moose Chandler in his office and Moose, a big man himself, hit him.

TWENTY-TWO

The next morning Clint was awakened by a pounding on his door. Gail sat up in bed next to him, holding the sheet up in front of her breasts.

"Who's that?"

"We'll never find out unless we ask," he said. "Didn't your pap tell you that?"

She made a face at him and he called out, "Who is it?"

"Turquette," came the answer. "If you want to do business with Mr. Chandler, you'd better come now."

"Let me get dressed," Clint shouted, and got out of bed.

Maybe Moose Chandler wasn't so ignorant about psychological tactics. Unless it was Turk's idea to wake him up early and catch him off guard.

"Where are you going?" Gail asked.

"I've got a business meeting," he said, pulling his pants on.

"Now?"

"Time is money in business," he said, slipping into a clean shirt.

"Should I get up?" she asked.

"No, no," he said, "you stay asleep—unless you have to get to work."

"I'm off this morning," she said.

"Then sleep," he said, bending over her and kissing her.

She grabbed his hand and placed it between her breasts.

"Are you coming back?"

"Sure I'm coming back," he said, running his hand over her left breast and cupping it. "I'll see you later, Gail."

"Okay."

He bent lower, kissed the nipple of her left breast, then took his gunbelt from the bedpost and strapped it on.

"Come on, Adams," Turk's voice called, accompanied by more pounding on the door.

"I'm coming."

Clint walked to the door, opened it and stepped out into the hall.

"You start your day early, don't you?"

Turk glared at him, obviously in a foul mood. The mottled bruise on the left side of his face probably wasn't doing anything to improve it.

"Are you ready to conduct business?" Turk demanded.

"I'm well rested," Clint said, "and ready."

Turk caught a look inside the room before Clint could pull the door shut, said, "Yeah," and led the way down the hall.

"My horse is in the livery," Clint said out on the street.

"Yeah," Turk said, "I'll meet you over there."

Clint walked to the livery and although Turk already had his horse, he didn't show up until Clint had Lance saddled.

"I'm ready," Clint said, riding Lance out.

Turk eyed Lancelot critically and tried to hide his admiration, unsuccessfully. Finally, he said, "Nice horse," grudgingly.

THE PANHANDLE SEARCH 95

"I've seen better," Clint said, looking Turk square in the eyes.

"Yeah," Turk said again. "Let's ride, Adams. The boss is waiting."

"Quite a bruise you've got there," Clint commented.

"So?"

"So nothing. I'd just like to see the guy that put it there, that's all."

"Let's ride," Turk said, and urged his horse into a gallop.

Following, Clint decided something was definitely eating at Turk today. Maybe Chandler had chewed him out, but he was still taking Clint to see Moose, and that was the whole idea.

It was almost a two hour ride to the Chandler spread, and when they finally reached it, Clint could see Chandler's brand on his front door, C with X over it.

He wouldn't take it too kindly if he were to find that brand—or any brand—on Duke. Clint had never branded Duke. He'd never seen any reason to. As angry as he was that Duke had been stolen, he'd be even angrier if he got him back marked up.

As if Moose Chandler didn't already have enough to answer for.

A hand came over and took the reins of their horses and Turk said, "Come inside."

They walked through the front door into a massive foyer and Turk said, "Wait here."

"Sure."

Turk went through a set of double doors, closing them behind him. The big man was gone only a few minutes, and then when he opened the doors again he stood aside and told Clint, "In here."

Clint walked in and saw Chandler seated behind his desk.

"Mr. Chandler," he said, approaching the desk.

"Mr. . . . Adams, is it?" Chandler said without looking up. "I believe you have some business you want to discuss with me?"

"That I do, Mr. Chandler," Clint said.

Chandler looked up and at first appeared not to recognize Clint. He was a good actor.

Finally, he said, "Don't I know you from somewhere?"

"You tried to buy a horse off of me in Wyoming a few weeks ago," Clint reminded him—as if the man needed any reminding.

"Now I remember," Chandler said. "A big black gelding, wasn't it?"

"That's right."

"Beautiful animal," Chandler said. "My offer still stands—or is that what you're here about?"

"That's not what I'm here about," Clint said. He removed Laura's letter from his pocket, handed it to Chandler and added, "This is."

Chandler took the letter, read it, then examined Clint closely.

"Miss Kennedy must trust you quite a bit to give you a letter of credit for this amount."

"Why shouldn't she?" Clint asked. "There are honest people in this world, Mr. Chandler . . . or don't you agree?"

"Oh, I agree, all right," Chandler said. "I certainly do."

"Then perhaps we can get on with our business."

Chandler looked at the letter again, and then put it down on his desk.

"May I have that back, please?" Clint asked.

"If we do business, you'll just be giving it back to me, Mr. Adams," Chandler reminded him.

"That's fine," Clint said. "I'll just hold onto it until we

agree that we are going to do business, if you don't mind."

"I don't mind," Chandler said, handing the letter back. "It just seems to me that a man worthy of such trust would show the same faith in others."

"I'm careful about who I trust, Mr. Chandler," Clint said, putting the letter away in his pocket.

"I see," Chandler said. "You're interested in a hundred head, is that right?"

"Prime stock," Clint added.

"I only deal in prime stock, Mr. Adams," Chandler told him. "I'll have Turk take you out and show you what we have."

"I'd really much rather have you show me, Chandler," Clint said.

"I assure you, Turk is an accomplished horseman—"

"That may be," Clint said, "but I want you."

He was tempted to draw his gun and point it at Chandler's nose, but he rarely drew his gun unless he was going to use it. Of course, there was always the chance that he *would* use it.

"Look, Adams—"

"I'm talking to your boss, Turk," Clint said without looking at the foreman. "Why don't you take a walk?"

"Listen, mister—" Turk began, but his boss cut him off.

"Go outside, Turk," he said. "I'll call you if I need you."

Clint could feel the tension in the air, but after a moment he heard Turk moving toward the doors, and then heard him close them.

"Does he know?" Clint asked.

"Does he know what, Mr. Adams?"

"That you stole my horse."

"I did?" Chandler asked, his face reflecting surprise. "That big black gelding?"

"That's the one," Clint said. "I've come to get him back."

Chandler craned his neck as if to see around Clint and then said, "I don't see the sheriff with you."

"That would be useless," Clint replied, "considering he's your man."

"This is very interesting, Mr. Adams—" Chandler started, but Clint cut him off.

"Let's don't play games with one another, Chandler," he said. "I want my horse back."

Chandler spread his hands and said, "I don't have him."

"I want to look around."

"Feel free."

"With you."

"I told you, Turk—"

"Don't make me insist, Chandler," Clint said, coldly.

Chandler studied the Gunsmith for a few moments, then rose, saying, "You've got a lot of gall coming here alone, Adams. How'd you get that letter?"

"Never mind that," Clint said. "Let's start with that nice big barn you've got behind your house."

"Whatever you say," Chandler replied. "We can go out the back way."

"Fine," Clint said, "lead the way."

Outside the house Chandler said, "You know, you really should be more careful with a horse like that, Adams. Losing your horse is bad enough, but losing one that fine—"

"Shut up."

Chandler shut up and conducted Clint to the barn. He opened the doors, and they walked in.

"Check every stall, if you like," Chandler invited, and that was just what Clint did.

Duke was nowhere in sight.

Pointing to the special stall Clint asked, "What's that stall for?"

THE PANHANDLE SEARCH 99

"That one? That's for problem horses, Adams. You know, the wild, unbreakable ones."

That's what Duke would have been, he thought. Wild and unridable. He wouldn't have let any of Chandler's men near him without trying to take his head off.

He walked to the stall, opened the door, and entered. It was empty, but had not been that way for long. From the droppings, he figured that there had been a horse in it sometime the night before. As he turned to leave his eye caught a stain on the floor of the stall, something dark.

It could have been blood.

He left the stall and confronted Chandler.

"If he's not here now, Chandler, he was," he said. "You've got him somewhere else."

"I'm telling you the truth, Adams," Chandler said. "I don't have your horse. Now if you don't get out of here, I'm going to have to send for the sheriff."

"Chandler—"

Chandler nodded his head slightly, and Clint heard a chilling sound from behind him.

The sound of the hammer of a gun being cocked.

"Turk," Chandler said, "would you get Mr. Adams's horse? He's leaving."

"It's out front, Mr. Chandler."

"Come on, Adams. I'll walk you to your horse."

Outside the barn, Lancelot was waiting for him.

"My God, Adams," Chandler said when he saw the white horse. "Where do you find them?"

Clint mounted up and threw Turk a glance. The big foreman was still holding his gun on him.

"Next time, Adams," Turk said, "without the guns."

"Anytime, Turk." Clint looked at Chandler and said, "This isn't finished, Chandler. I'm going to get my horse, and then I'm going to get you."

"Maybe I should just have Turk kill you now, then," Chandler said, "to avoid future problems."

Clint looked at Turk then, and wondered if this would be it. Would he be able to draw and fire before the big man could pull the trigger?

"Get going, Adams," Chandler said, breaking the tense silence in the air. "If you're going to come back with some more wild accusations, make sure you've got the law with you, or I'll let Turk kill you."

Clint was burning with rage and frustration as he turned Lance around and started away. His back itched, waiting for a bullet to punch through him, but none came and eventually he was out of range.

Chandler and Turk watched Clint Adams until he was out of sight, and then Turk holstered his gun and turned to his boss.

"You should have let me kill him when we had the chance, Moose," he said, but Chandler wasn't really listening. He was feeling very satisfied with himself.

"So that was the Gunsmith, huh?" he asked his foreman. "He ain't much, is he?"

Turk looked at Moose, who was smiling for the first time in weeks, and said, "Don't you believe it."

TWENTY-THREE

Clint rode back to town at a leisurely pace, remembering the route Turk had followed. He was trying to give himself time to cool off. Damn! How had he let Turk get the drop on him so easily in the barn? Was he that worried about Duke? Getting himself killed wasn't going to get the big boy back for him, so he was going to have to keep a tighter rein on himself if he was going to get Duke back.

He made it to town, even though he halfway expected to be shot out of the saddle.

It was afternoon by the time Clint rode back into town. He dropped Lance off at the livery and walked right to the saloon for a drink.

"Whiskey," he told the bartender. The man had no sooner put the drink down in front of him than Clint picked it up and drained it. "Now I want a cold beer." The bartender gave him the beer and Clint took it to a corner table. He sat sipping it while the whiskey tried to burn a hole in his stomach.

All right, he told himself, so Moose Chandler has moved Duke somewhere. Chandler only owned half of Texas, right?

How hard could it be to find Duke on Chandler's land?

Alone.

Well, at least the blood in that special stall told Clint that Chandler and his men weren't having an easy time of it with his big black buddy. He hoped that Duke was biting a few more hands and splitting a few heads.

Chandler had definitely come out ahead in this, their second go-round, but that might work to Clint's advantage. The rancher might tend to underestimate the Gunsmith now, perhaps feeling that Clint's reputation was exaggerated.

Turk was a different story. Clint remembered the look in Turk's eyes when he was holding a gun on him. The foreman had wanted to pull the trigger, but his boss hadn't let him. No doubt Turk felt that was a mistake.

Clint was looking forward to proving that he was right.

He was working on his second beer, and finally getting to the point where he could think about the morning without wanting to fire his gun into the wall, when the kid, Jed, walked into the saloon. He looked around the room, spotted Clint, and approached his table.

"You supposed to keep closer tabs on me this morning?" Clint asked.

"I'm here on my own, Mr. Adams," the kid said. "I got fired yesterday."

"Oh," Clint said. "Listen, I'm sorry, kid—"

"That's all right," Jed said, cutting him off. "I wasn't real happy there, anyway."

"Pull up a chair, kid," Clint said. "Are you old enough to drink?"

"I'll have a beer," Jed said, seemingly unaffected by the question.

Clint waved to the bartender and indicated that he wanted another beer. The man brought it over without complaining, threw a nervous look Clint's way, and went back behind the bar.

"Have a drink, kid," Clint said. "We've got something in common."

"What's that?"

"We're both unhappy with the Chandler spread."

"Well, in your case," Jed said, "I think I can help you."

"Oh, yeah?" Clint asked. "How?"

"I told you that I had heard some talk about a big black horse from some of the boys who had seen him."

"Yeah?"

"Well, I heard something else," Jed said.

"What?" Clint said, prompting him. For a moment he thought the kid was going to hold out the information for money.

"Your horse killed somebody last night, and ran off," Jed finally said.

"He what?"

"He's gone. He's not at the ranch anymore."

"Is this reliable information?" Clint asked.

"I heard it from one of the men who was there," Jed said. "He told me this morning, when I was clearing out my things."

Clint remembered the blood on the floor of the stall, and it all fit. Duke was no longer at the Chandler ranch because he had finally found an opportunity to break free.

And he had killed a man doing it!

If Chandler wanted to, he could have the sheriff round up a posse and go out searching for Duke, claiming he was simply a horse who had turned mankiller.

If that were the case, they'd kill Duke.

"Kid, you want a job?" Clint asked, putting down his beer.

"Sure."

"You know the area?"

"Like it was home."

"All right," Clint said, getting up.

Jed stared at his beer, which he'd barely touched, and asked, "Where are we going?"

"Hunting," Clint said. "We've got to find Duke before anybody else does, Jed, or he might not live very much longer."

TWENTY-FOUR

The battle was very brief.

Duke's size, and the fact that he was older than his foe, worked in his favor.

When he had first come across the herd of wild horses, Duke had been wary, but even an animal realizes that there is safety in numbers, and if Duke joined the herd, he would be all that much harder to find. He did not want the men from the ranch finding him and trying to force him to go back.

Duke ran down into the valley where the horses were grazing, and almost immediately he was confronted by the leader of the herd, which consisted of about twenty-five horses.

The leader was a big, three-year-old palomino who immediately resented the presence of the larger, older Duke, and wasted no time in issuing a challenge.

Either fight, or leave.

Duke chose to fight, and the battle was brief. Although the palomino was wild and Duke had lived among men for the better part of his life, it was really no contest. Duke had learned much about survival, and he gave the younger horse a lesson in how it's done.

When the fight was over, the former leader was battered and bruised, but Duke made no move to force the horse to leave the company of the herd. All the palomino had to do was accept Duke as the new leader, and he did.

Duke quickly asserted himself by taking the herd out of the valley, with intentions of leading them as far away from man as possible. He didn't want any of them going through what he recently had.

The scent of man—and man's blood—was all too fresh in his nostrils.

TWENTY-FIVE

Clint took Jed to his hotel room, where he paid the boy some money to work for him for at least two days as a guide, and then gave him money to use for supplies. Clint hoped that they'd be able to locate Duke within those two days. Not knowing what Chandler's plans were now that Duke had killed one of his men, Clint didn't want to take much longer than that.

"Do you want me to go out and buy these supplies now?" Jed asked.

Clint saw the look on his face and said, "Why don't you have lunch first, Jed, and then buy the supplies?"

"Right, boss," the kid said, happily.

"We'll leave as soon as you get the supplies," Clint said.

"What? I thought we'd leave in the morning."

"You can get us someplace to camp before dark, can't you?" Clint asked.

"Uh, sure, there's a couple of places I know of, but—"

"Then we'll leave today," Clint said, "as soon as you

have lunch and pick up the supplies. You got a good horse?"

"Yeah, but—"

"Then go have lunch. I'll meet you back here in an hour."

"What should I buy?"

"Buy whatever you like," Clint said.

"I was talking about the supplies," Jed said, "not about my lunch."

"That's what I'm talking about, too," Clint assured him. "Now get going!"

"What are you going to be doing?"

"I think I'll go over and visit the doctor and the undertaker," Clint said.

"You sick?" Jed asked. "Or worse?"

"Neither," Clint said. "I just want to ask a few questions. Come on, I'll walk you down. You look like you might collapse if you don't eat in the next ten minutes."

While Jed was feeding his face and collecting supplies, Clint went out to try and find out if anyone knew anything about a man being killed by a horse at the Chandler ranch.

The doctor, a cantankerous old coot who smelled like he bathed in booze, didn't know anything about it. Clint went into the doctor's office complaining of a pain somewhere, but once inside he mentioned that he'd heard something about a man being killed by a horse.

"Don't know nothin' about that," the doctor said, probing Clint's back. "Where'd you say that pain was?"

"Uh, around the right side, I guess," Clint replied. "You mean nobody was brought into you suffering from some kind of an injury, maybe a head wound?"

"Nope," the doctor said. "Is it here?" he asked, pushing on Clint's side.

"Well, maybe it was the left side," Clint said.

Probing the left side the doctor said, "Besides, if he was dead, he wouldn't be brought to me. He'd go to the undertaker."

"Yeah," Clint said, "I know."

"Is it here?"

"You know what?" Clint said, standing up and slipping his shirt back on. "I can't remember where that pain was now. I'll come back when I do, though."

"Write it down, next time," the doctor said, uncorking a bottle of whiskey, "so's I don't have to look all over for it."

"What'd you say this fella's name was?" the undertaker asked. His name was Fortescue, and he was a roly-poly man who would have looked more at home running a café.

"Cutter," Clint said, "Tom Cutter. I represent his family, and we're trying to locate him. He was last heard from in this area, and I was just wondering if perhaps he had, uh, gotten sick, or been injured and died."

The undertaker thought a moment, rubbing his jaw, and then said, "Well, I ain't had anybody by that name in the past few months, that I can remember."

"Do you have anyone here now?" Clint asked. "Perhaps if I took a look—"

"You like looking at bodies?" the undertaker asked.

"No, but if he was brought in under another name, I might be able to recognize him."

"Well, the only fella I got in here right now is called Sykes. He's from the Chandler ranch."

"Oh?" Clint asked. "What happened to him?"

"Took a fall and cracked his head open," Fortescue said. "You want to take a look and see if he's your man?"

"Why not?"

The undertaker took Clint into the back room, where the

man was lying nude on a table.

"Here," Fortescue said. He tilted the man's face towards Clint, but not before the Gunsmith had seen the open wound on the back of the man's head.

He had seen such wounds before, on men who had been struck in the head by a horse's hoof.

"Is that your man?"

Clint almost said yes, because in reality it was, but he said, "No, that's not him. Thanks anyway."

"Sure," the undertaker said. "I hope you find who you're looking for."

"Yes," Clint said, "so do I."

"I can't spare any men to go out and look for that—that—"

"Devil?" Moose Chandler asked Turk, who seemed to be at a loss for words.

"That's what you call him," Turk said, "but I think that's what he really is."

"All right," Moose Chandler said, making a decision he hadn't wanted to make. "You're convinced that this Gunsmith is more dangerous than he's shown, right?"

"Definitely," Turk said. "He could cost you everything you've got, Moose."

"And you."

"I don't intend for that to happen," Turk said.

"All right," Moose said, "neither do I. You take Barron, Doran and Watson out and you find that horse."

"And?"

"And kill it," Chandler said. "He's a mankiller now. It would be impossible to break him now, anyway. We've got to get rid of him. Maybe after we do Adams will give up and leave."

"And if he doesn't?"

"It will bring a lot more heat killing him than killing the horse," Chandler said, "but if we have to, we will."

"All right," Turk said, clapping his big hands together. "All right!"

As he left Moose Chandler's office, the whole business had taken on a new light for Turk. If he could kill Adams, the legendary Gunsmith, he'd make a name and rep for himself, and then he wouldn't have to work for Moose Chandler—or anyone—ever again.

This was one chance he did not want to blow.

Turk sent a man out to the lineshack to pick up Lefty Barron, One-Eye Doran and Roy Watson. When they got back, he spoke to them in the bunkhouse.

"What's this all about, Turk," One-Eye Doran asked, "not that I'm complaining. I'm kind of tired of staying out of sight."

"Yeah," Lefty Barron said, "we took care of this fella once, we can do it again."

"You're all idiots," Turk said. "Do you know who this fella really is?"

"It don't matter—" Doran began, but Roy Watson cut him off.

"Quiet, Orville," he said.

"Don't call me that," Doran said. He hated when Watson, or anyone, called him by his given name.

The three men had been hired at the same time, and although Turk was the foreman, Watson always seemed to be the one the other two listened to.

"Who is he, Turk?" Watson asked.

"Clint Adams," Turk said. "They call him the Gunsmith."

The three men fell silent and exchanged unreadable looks.

"Well, what do you know," Lefty Barron finally said. "You know, he killed a one-armed sheriff over in Palmerville, Wyoming a while back." Raising his empty cuff Doran said, "I kind of feel like he killed one of my own. I'd like a shot at the famous Gunsmith."

"You're crazy," Doran said, running the ball of his right index finger over his patch.

"You're all going to get a shot at him," Turk said.

"What do you mean?" Watson asked.

Turk relayed the orders he'd gotten from Moose Chandler.

"He didn't say anything about killing the Gunsmith," Watson pointed out, "just the horse."

"No, killing Adams is my idea," Turk said. "I have a hankering to make a better life for myself, boys. How do you feel about that?"

"Always looking for something better," Lefty Barron said, and the other two nodded.

"No qualms about killing a man?"

"It's been done before," One-Eye Doran said.

"Besides," Barron said, "Clint Adams is already a dead man."

"How do you figure that?" Watson asked.

"He lives by his gun, don't he?" Barron asked. "Men like that usually catch a bullet."

"Like Hickok," Doran said.

"Right," Barron said.

"All right," Turk said, "then we're agreed."

"How are we going to get him?"

"We'll go out looking for the horse," Turk said, "and we'll find Adams."

"How do you figure?"

"He'll be out there looking for his horse," Turk said, "same as us."

THE PANHANDLE SEARCH   113

"What makes you say that?" Watson asked. "He still thinks Chandler has the horse."

"No," Turk said, "he doesn't. He knows that the horse got away last night."

"How does he know that?" Watson asked.

"He knows," Turk said, "because I sent him a message telling him so."

Clint met Jed at the hotel and told him to go to the livery, rent a packhorse and load him up for the trip.

"I'll meet you there."

"Okay, boss," Jed said.

"Did you eat enough for lunch, Jed?" Clint asked.

"I sure did," Jed said, "but you know what? I'm getting hungry again, already."

"I don't know where you put it," Clint said, examining the boy's bony frame, "but when we camp, you can pack in some more."

"Right, boss."

"And stop calling me boss," Clint said. "The name is Clint."

"All right, Clint," Jed said. He was obviously impressed by the fact that he was being allowed to call the Gunsmith by his first name.

Clint went up to his room to collect his saddlebags and rifle, and found Gail waiting for him.

"How'd you get in?" he asked.

"I work here, remember?" she said.

"That answers that," Clint said. "Why are you in here?" he asked, then crossed the room to where his saddlebags rested on a chair.

"I heard the boy in the dining room say you were leaving today," she said. "I thought I'd come up and say goodbye."

"Well, it's true that I'm leaving," he said, "but not for good. I'll be back in a few days, at the most."

He hoped.

"Where are you going?"

He looked at her, groping for an answer she could accept, and then said, "Hunting."

"Oh," she said, looking relieved. "I thought you were leaving town . . . without saying good-bye."

"I wouldn't do that, Gail," he assured her.

"I think I knew that," she said.

"Good."

"Still . . ."

"Still what?" he asked, facing her with his saddlebags and rifle in hand.

Her hands were at the buttons of her high-necked dress as she said, "I did come up here to say good-bye in a specific way."

"Is that so?" he asked. She opened her dress and the slopes of her creamy breasts came into view. She undid the buttons on her undergarment, and her large breasts burst into view, with their pink-tipped nipples already hardening.

"It would be a shame to waste it," she said, "don't you think?"

She moved close to him so that the tips of her breasts prodded his chest, and he dropped his saddlebags to the floor, and placed his rifle on the chair next to them.

"I think," he said, palming her breasts, "it would be a terrible shame."

He kissed her then and undid the remainder of her buttons so that she could slip out of her clothes. Then he slipped out of his and pushed her back towards the bed. When the back of her knees struck the mattress she fell onto it, and Clint went with her.

THE PANHANDLE SEARCH

"Oh," she moared as he tongued her nipples and, "God!" she finished as he took them in his teeth.

He let one hand slip between them and, finding her moist and ready, slid two fingers inside of her and wiggled them around.

"Oh, yes," she cried, "yes, yes, yes . . ."

With his thumb he found her stiff button of love and rotated it while he continued to move his fingers inside of her, and she went wild beneath him.

"Oh, please, Clint, please," she cried, "I want you inside of me . . ."

He removed his hand, moved one leg over her and slid into her very slowly. She moved her hips up, as if trying to swallow him up faster, and when he was firmly planted she began rotating her hips almost uncontrollably. Once again he slid his hands beneath her to cup her ample buttocks and control the pace.

"Oh," she said, her eyes widening as he drove into her. "Oh, Jesus, I can't—It's almost more than I can— Oh, Clint, yes, don't ever stop. If you try and stop I'll . . ." She dug her nails into his back so that he couldn't get away and lifted them both off the bed with her feet planted firmly on the mattress.

As he felt her belly begin to tremble—the sign in many women that they are about to come—he drove himself even deeper and released a flood inside of her.

"Ahhh . . ." she moaned, as her insides began to milk him for more and more.

He kissed her then and she thrust her tongue hungrily into his mouth, found his and began to chew on it. As the spasms inside of her subsided, she lowered her hips to the bed and he slid his hands away from her buttocks to the small of her back.

"Oh, Lord," she said, sliding her mouth away from his. "That was incredible."

"Yes," he said, "it was. That should keep me warm for a few days."

"Until you get back, you mean."

"Right," he agreed, "until I come back. Which reminds me." He got out of bed and said, "Jed will be waiting for me. I've got to get going, Gail."

"That's okay," she said, stretching on the bed. "The faster you leave, the quicker you'll get back."

"Yeah," he said, dressing and admiring the fullness of her body, "there is that."

"Maybe," she said, reversing her position on the bed so that she was lying on her belly, "I've even given you a little reason to come back earlier than you planned?"

"Well," he agreed, "plans do have a way of changing from time to time."

He picked up his saddlebags and rifle again and walked to the door. Before leaving he turned to her and said, "You never know."

When he got over to the livery Jed wasn't there yet—or had been there and gone—so he went inside and saddled Lance himself.

"We're going on a hunting trip, big fella," he told the white horse, "and if we're successful, you'll be going home."

The horse eyed him once, then turned and looked away. In a way Clint was sorry that he had no use for two saddle horses. He couldn't ride anyone but Duke, and Lance just wouldn't do to pull his rig.

"You're going to have to go back," he said, "until someone else comes along who strikes your fancy."

When he mounted up and rode Lance out, Jed was waiting

there, astride his horse and leading a pack horse. If he was annoyed at having to wait he forgot it when his eyes fell on Lancelot.

"Golly," he said, "with a horse like that, why are you so interested in getting the other one back?"

"You'll know when you see him, kid," Clint said. "Come on, let's go hunting."

TWENTY-SIX

Jed led the way out of town and Clint ambled along behind with Lance.

"Have you picked out someplace for us to camp?" Clint asked.

Jed turned in his saddle and said, "Yeah, and it's someplace where we won't be spotted by any of the XC crew."

"That's good. I'm hoping that we're getting a head start on them."

"Do you really think—" Jed started to ask, but Clint stopped him.

"Wait a minute," he said. He rode up alongside of Jed so that the kid wouldn't get a stiff neck. "All right."

"Do you really think that they'll go out looking for him?" Jed asked. "I mean, he's caused enough trouble already, hasn't he?"

"They'll go after him for one of two reasons," Clint explained. "Either Moose simply won't let him get away, or he'll have to have him killed."

"Killed? But why?"

THE PANHANDLE SEARCH

"Maybe he thinks it will get me off his back," Clint said. "Or maybe he'll do it just because Duke killed one of his men."

"Duke? Is that what you call your horse?"

"Yeah."

"You must think a lot of him to go through all this."

"I do. We've been together for a while."

"Like partners?"

"Just like partners," Clint said.

"Why are we going out now?" Lefty Barron complained to Roy Watson, as they saddled their horses.

"Because Turk thinks that Adams won't waste any time getting out there, and he wants to find the horse before he does."

"And kill it?"

"And watch it," Watson said. "We'll wait for Adams to watch it, and then take care of both of them at the same time."

"What do you think of Turk, Roy?" Barron asked.

"What do you mean?"

"He means are you afraid of him," One-Eye Doran said.

"Why? Because he's big?" Watson said. "If I was going to be afraid of every big man I met, I'd be afraid of you two." Both Doran and Barron were taller than Watson, who was only five seven. However, both of the other men knew that Watson was a terror with his fists, and also that he was smarter than both of them. That was why they never argued about who the leader was.

"You fellas both know I ain't afraid of you."

"And what about Moose Chandler?" Barron asked.

"Chandler pays my salary right now," Roy Watson said. "That makes him the best friend I've got, don't it?"

The three of them were laughing when Turk came into the barn.

"What's so funny?" he asked.

Watson looked at him and said, "Oh, we were just discussing who our best friends are."

Turk frowned at them and then said, "Well, forget that and keep your minds on business."

Turk went to saddle his own horse and Watson exchanged glances with his two friends and said, "That's just what we're doing."

TWENTY-SEVEN

When Jed and Clint reached their campsite Clint felt that he had made the right choice in hiring the boy to be his guide.

"This is perfect," Clint said.

"Yeah, I figured it would be," Jed said.

It was a rock shelf on the side of a hill that was virtually a cave, except that it was more open and allowed more light inside. They wouldn't need a fire for light until it got dark.

"Where does Chandler's land start?" he asked Jed.

"Right above us," Jed said. "They can't see us from up there, or from the bottom. The only way anyone would find us is to look for us here."

"Well," Clint said, dismounting, "let's hope that they don't do that. Is there room inside for the horses?"

"Yeah, farther back," Jed said. "It'll be dark soon. I can gather up some stuff for a fire if you want to take care of the horses."

Slightly taken aback by the boy's sudden take-charge attitude, Clint said, "Fine, go ahead."

They'd seen no sign of Duke, or any horse, up until this point, but then Jed said that they shouldn't hope to. He felt they'd have more luck farther into Chandler's land, and Clint agreed. More and more he was starting to realize that the farther away from people Jed got, the more self-sufficient and confident he got. The kid was going to prove an asset in the search for Duke, of that he was sure.

Clint had all the horses unsaddled—and unpacked—by the time Jed returned, and rubbed Lance down while Jed built a fire.

"Can you cook?" he asked.

"Yeah," Jed said. "I can cook what I like."

"And what's that?"

"Bacon, beans, coffee—"

"You've got the job," Clint said. "Will the smell of bacon and coffee in the air bring anyone running to take a look?"

"Naw," Jed said. "We ain't on anybody's land. Nobody's gonna come looking."

"Good," Clint said.

Clint settled down on the ground, leaning against his saddle, and watched Jed cook. The kid put plenty of coffee in the pot, so Clint knew that would be okay. As long as he didn't burn the bacon, eating should be no problem over the next couple of days.

When Jed passed him a plate it had bacon strips, beans and a chunk of bread on it, and it looked fine.

"There you go," Jed said. "I hope you don't get tired of this over the next two days."

"I doubt it," Clint said. "What I eat doesn't really matter, as long as I have enough strength and energy to keep looking for Duke."

He tasted the modest meal and nodded his approval.

THE PANHANDLE SEARCH

"It's fine, Jed."

Obviously pleased, Jed said, "Thanks . . . Clint." Maybe, he was thinking, he just could get used to calling the Gunsmith by his first name.

"Could I ask you something?" Jed said then.

"Sure."

"It's personal."

"If I think it's too personal I'll let you know," Clint promised.

"How does it feel . . . being a—I mean, having a reputation like you have?"

He'd been asked that before, and he always gave the same answer. "It feels lousy, Jed. But no one ever believes that. Young fellows like yourself think it's exciting to have a reputation, but it's not. It's more exciting not having one, and wishing you did."

"Did you ever wish for one?"

"No," Clint said. "I just tried to do my job the best way I knew how, and I had a natural ability with guns. I wasn't looking for a rep, Jed, and I'm damned sorry I've got one. It's kept me from leading a normal—and probably happier—life."

"Golly," Jed said. "I never thought about it like that."

"Are you looking for a reputation, Jed?" Clint asked.

Jed laughed and, holding up his plate, said, "Maybe as a cook, but not as a gunman. No, Clint, I'm not looking for a reputation. I was just wondering, that's all. You want some coffee now?"

"Sure."

Jed poured out two cups of strong coffee and handed one to Clint.

"Good and strong," Clint said after a sip. "Just the way I like it."

"What are you gonna do to Mr. Chandler when you get your horse back?" Jed asked. "Or if you don't get your horse back?"

Clint looked at Jed then, and held out his plate. "That one's too personal, Jed. How about some more chow?"

Later, Jed told Clint about a valley that was frequented by herds of wild horses.

"There's good grazing there," he said. "We can ride over there come morning and check it out. If there aren't any horses there tomorrow, we can ride down and look around, maybe find out when they were there last."

"Sounds like you've got it all figured out," Clint said.

"That's what you hired me for, ain't it?" Jed asked. "To take you to the right places?"

"That's right," Clint said. "That, and cooking."

Jed laughed, and got up to go and clean the plates off. Before leaving, though, he turned and asked another question.

"Clint?"

"Yeah?"

"Do you think your horse could hook up with a herd of wild ones after being around men for so long?"

Clint thought about it, then laughed and said, "Jed, I'll bet that if he came across a herd of wild horses he's their leader by now."

TWENTY-EIGHT

"How did you figure this?" Watson asked Turk, staring down at the herd of wild horses. In front of the herd was a magnificent black horse, which he—and the others—knew only too well.

"I can pick him off from here real easy," One-Eye Doran said. He took out his rifle, holding it in his left hand. His right hand was still bandaged as a result of the bite of the big horse. Doran itched to put the horse down.

"Put up that rifle," Turk said. He did not notice that Doran looked first at Watson, who nodded, before he put the rifle away.

"I'm a horseman, Watson," Turk said. "I know horses. I knew what this one would do even before he did."

"You read horse's minds?" Lefty Barron asked.

"That's exactly it," Turk said. "There are enough wild bunches running around here that I knew he'd run into one. That horse," he said, pointing to the black who was only a hundred yards away from them, "would never join a herd of horses and follow a leader. No, that son of a buck would have

125

to be the leader, and then he'd take them as far away from us as he could."

"You make him sound almost human," Watson said. "He's just a horse, ain't he?"

"If he was, would a man like Clint Adams be going through all this trouble to get him back?" Turk asked. "And would Moose Chandler have stolen him? A man who had never stolen anything before in his life—to hear him tell it. Look at him, Watson," Turk said, ignoring the other two. "Does that look like just another horse to you?"

Watson looked down at the proud gelding and had to admit, he did look rather special.

"I still think I should put him down now," One-Eye said, flexing his injured hand. He could still feel the horse's sharp teeth digging into his flesh.

"You'll get your chance," Turk promised, "but don't take that rifle out again until I say so. Got it?"

Doran looked at Watson, and this time Turk caught it.

"Don't be looking at Watson, One-Eye," Turk said. "When I tell you something you'd better damn well listen. That goes for you, too, Lefty."

"What did I do?"

"Nothing, yet," Turk said. He looked at Watson and said, "We have to have a talk, Roy."

"When?"

"We'll camp on that ridge, so we can watch the herd. Adams should be along before long. We'll talk up there."

"Okay," Watson said, shrugging. "Lead the way."

"Up the hill, boys," Turk told Lefty and One-Eye. He didn't want either man behind him, and brought up the rear with Roy Watson.

Turk hoped he wasn't going to have too much trouble right here even before Clint Adams showed up.

* * *

"What did you want to talk about?" Roy Watson asked. He and Turk were alone now, while Lefty and One-Eye were taking care of the horses.

"I think you know," Turk said.

"Them?"

"Maybe them," Turk said, "maybe all of you."

"You don't have to worry about me, Turk," Watson said.

"No, huh?" Turk said. "You're the only one I really worry about, Roy, because you've got brains."

"Maybe you ought to get to the point," Watson said.

"There's something in this for all of us, Roy," Turk said. "I want you to keep those two friends of yours in line. I don't want to catch a bullet in the back, and I don't want to have to kill either one of them."

"Why would you have to do that?"

"They're your men," Turk said. "I've known that since I hired the three of you. Those two like to kill, but you keep them in check."

"You don't think I like to kill?"

"Sure you do," Turk said. "But you know when; they don't. Look, damn it, this is the Gunsmith we're talking about. If we make a wrong move, he's gonna kill all four of us. If we make a right move, it could mean big things for all of us."

"And you know the right move?"

"Right," Turk said. "What do you say?"

Watson seemed to turn it over in his mind before giving his answer.

"I'll try and keep a tight rein on them, Turk," Watson said. "Although I don't know how long I can do that."

"It won't have to be long," Turk promised. "We take care of Clint Adams, and his horse, and then we go our own way."

"You go back to Chandler's ranch?"

"I go my own way, Roy," Turk said. "You and your friends go yours."

"We got pay coming, Turk," Watson reminded him.

"I'll see that you get it," Turk said. "I'll see that the three of you get just what's coming to you. Trust me."

TWENTY-NINE

"This is the valley I was talking about last night," Jed said.

Clint nodded, stood up in his saddle to take a good, long look. The valley was beautiful, good grazing land, as Jed had said, but at the moment it was empty.

"Let's go down," Clint suggested.

"Right."

They rode down a steep incline to the floor of the valley, and rode around a bit, so Jed could look around.

"There was a herd here yesterday sometime," Jed announced after a few moments.

"Are you sure?"

"And Duke got away the night before."

"Right."

"Can you trail them?"

"Do you think your horse is with them?" Jed asked.

"I think we should find them and find out," Clint said, "don't you?"

"Yes, sir," Jed said. "I'll find them for you."

"Let's get going, then."

As Jed started off, Clint looked around again. According to Jed, this valley was not far from Chandler's ranch. Duke could have run this way during the night, and come upon the herd the next morning. If Duke had taken control of the herd, he'd most likely lead them away from the men who had been cruel to him, and imprisoned him.

As close as he and Duke had been over the years, Clint started to worry. What if the big gelding suddenly took to the life of a wild horse? Could Clint get him to accept things the way they had been before Moose Chandler took a hand?

The only way he was going to find out the answer to that question was to find Duke. That was the first priority, find him and make sure he was in good health. If, after that, he felt that Duke didn't want to come back, that was fine, too. He didn't own Duke. They were partners, and partners had been known to go their separate ways before.

Duke sensed the presence of the men before he saw them. He sent a message through the herd for everyone to be ready to follow him. The men only seemed to be watching the herd, but the moment they made a move towards them, Duke would be off and running, with the entire herd behind him.

He stood tall and unmoving while the others milled about, keeping his eyes on the men up on the ridge. There was only one man whose presence he would welcome, and he instinctively knew that he was not one of them.

He watched, and waited.

"That horse gives me the creeps," One-Eye Doran said to the others.

"Why is that?" Watson asked.

"He just stands there, watching us. I get the feeling he's watching me."

THE PANHANDLE SEARCH 131

"Maybe he liked what he tasted back in Little Creek," Lefty Barron suggested.

Doran made a fist with his wounded hand and said, "Well, he'll never get the chance to try it again. That's a promise."

"He really looks worried," Barron said, looking down at the big black.

"Devil," Turk said in a low voice.

"What?" Watson said.

"That's what Chandler called him," Turk answered. "Devil."

"It suits him," Watson said.

"I wonder what the Gunsmith calls him?" Lefty Barron said.

"When I get finished with that animal," One-Eye Doran said, taking his gun out of his holster, "all he's gonna answer to is *dead*."

After Clint left, Gail fell into a depression and she thought that this would be a good time to go and see her father. She went to the livery, saddled her horse, and rode out to the XC Ranch.

Gail Chandler had moved off the ranch two years before, and gotten her job at the hotel. She loved her father, John "Moose" Chandler, but wanted to be independent of him. He didn't like the idea of her working in town, but had come to accept the situation, as long as she agreed to come out and see him from time to time.

This time, she picked the wrong time.

"You what?" Moose Chandler bellowed at his daughter, who flinched inadvertently.

"I've met a man," she said.

"I heard that part," Chandler said. "What did you say his name was?"

"Clint," she said. "Clint Adams."

"Gail," he said, rising from his desk and walking around it to take his daughter's shoulders in his big hands, "listen to me. You are not to see that man anymore."

"What are you talking about?" she demanded. "Of course I'll see him again."

"No, you won't. I forbid it."

"Father," she said patiently, "you forbade me to leave home, too."

"Damn it, girl!" he shouted, squeezing her shoulders harder than he intended.

"You're hurting me," she said, attempting to twist out of his grip.

He let her shoulders go as if they had suddenly become scalding hot.

"Listen to me, baby," he said. "You don't know who this man is."

"Of course I don't," she said. "I just met him, but I'll get to know him."

In spite of her father's blowup, Gail felt a sense of great relief. She knew that Turk had seen her in Clint's bed, and it was obvious that he hadn't told her father . . . yet.

"Gail, I know this man," Chandler said. "He's a killer."

"That's ridiculous."

"They call him the Gunsmith," Chandler went on, desperately. "Surely you've heard of him."

"The Gunsmith?" she said. She had heard that name before, of course, but Clint? The Gunsmith?

"Father, are you sure we're talking about the same man?" she asked.

"Of course, I'm sure," he said. "I should know, since the man is after me—"

"After you?"

"Yes, of course," Chandler said suddenly, as if he understood something now. "That's why he took up with you, to get to me."

"That's ridiculous," she said. "Don't you think I'm capable of attracting a man on my own? He didn't even know I was your daughter. I never told him my last name."

"That's got to be it . . ." Chandler went on, turning away from his daughter.

"Father, you're not listening!"

"He dared to use my own daughter against me," Chandler said, bringing his fist down on the desk top. "I'm glad I sent them out there, now."

"Sent who out where?" Gail asked. "Father, what's going on. Is Clint in trouble?"

"Not yet," he answered, feeling pleased with himself, "but he will be. If he finds that horse at the same time Turk and the others do—"

"You sent Turk out after Clint?"

Suddenly, Chandler realized that he may have said too much in the presence of his daughter.

"Listen, honey, it's nothing for you to worry about—" he began, moving toward her again, but she backed away from him.

"Something's going on that I don't understand," she said, "but I understand Turk. You sent him out to kill Clint, didn't you?"

"No, of course not," he said. "Turk's not a hired killer, for God's sake."

"I've got to find him," she said, starting for the door. "I've got to find Clint."

"Gail!" Chandler shouted. "Don't you dare go out that door."

She stopped at the door and glared back at her father defiantly.

"Don't go out that door," he said again.

"Father," she said, wearily, "you told me the same thing two years ago."

"And you left anyway," he said. "I forgave you that, Gail."

"But you won't forgive me this? Is that it?"

"I'm trying to save you from making a fool of yourself," he said. "The man cares nothing for you."

"You're wrong," she said, "and I'm going to find him and prove it to you."

"Gail—" he shouted again, but she was out the door. He ran after her, but when he got outside, she was astride her horse and riding away.

"Damn you, girl," he said, "damn you and your mother's stubborn streak." He turned to one of his hands, who had been standing by Gail Chandler's horse, and said, "Get my horse."

THIRTY

"We're getting closer," Jed said as the day wore on, and the closer they got to finding this particular herd, the more jumpy Clint got. He was anxious to find out if Duke was with them.

"We're going to have to move carefully, Jed," he warned. "If Chandler's got men out looking for Duke, we might run into them, and they're not going to welcome us with open arms."

"I'm ready," the boy said. He wore no sidearm, but he had a well-worn rifle which he put his hand on to indicate his readiness.

"Where'd you get that old Henry?" Clint asked.

"It was my pa's," Jed said. "It's the only thing he left me when he died."

"You know how to use it?"

"I sure do," Jed said. "I can shoot the hind legs off a fly at a hundred yards."

If he lived up to half that brag, Jed was going to prove even handier to have around than Clint had originally thought.

"You don't like being around a lot of people much, do you?" Clint asked.

"How can you tell?"

"You're a lot different out here than you are in town, as if all those people intimidate you."

"Well, you're right," Jed said. "I don't like to be around a lot of people. That's why I wasn't happy with my job at the Chandler ranch. My folks were mountain people, and we never saw a lot of other folks around when I was growing up. I didn't even have no brothers and sisters, and my maw died when I was young, so it was just me and Pa, until he up and died a couple of years ago."

"Sounds like maybe you ought to just go back on up into the mountains, Jed."

"I just might do that, Clint, after this is all over with," Jed said. "If there are more people out there like One-Eye Doran and Lefty Barron—"

"Lefty Barron?" Clint asked. "They wouldn't call him Lefty because he's missing a hand, would they?"

"That's him," Jed said, "and that missing hand makes him as mean as hell. Do you know him?"

"We've met," Clint said, "briefly. He and a couple of friends of his are the ones who took Duke from me."

"How'd they do that . . . to you?" Jed asked curiously.

"From behind," Clint said. "Two of them faced me, and one of them hit me from behind."

"I'm surprised they didn't just kill you."

"They might have, if they had known who I was," Clint said. "Anyway, I heard from the liveryman there that Duke took a piece out of one of their hands—in fact, he said the fella was wearing a patch."

"That's One-Eye," Jed said. "He's been sporting a bandage on his hand and I wondered where it came from."

"Lefty Barron and One-Eye Doran," Clint said. "Who's the third one?"

"Roy Watson," Jed said. "He's the smart one. The other two are bigger and stronger, but Roy's smarter . . . and meaner. The other two listen to what he says."

"What about Turk?"

"Turk's the foreman, but I think even he knows that One-Eye and Lefty are Roy's men."

Clint looked around, with a funny feeling nudging at him.

"What's the matter?"

"I just have the feeling that if Turk is out here looking for Duke, he'll have those three with him."

If that were true, it made the situation much more dangerous. He'd be facing killers, and not ranch hands. Still, he owed those three something, and out here was just as good a place as any to pay it back. After that was done, only Moose Chandler would be left.

"Are you gonna kill them?" Jed asked.

Startled, Clint looked at the kid and said, "Why do you ask that?"

"The look on your face," Jed said. "It's scary."

"I'm not planning to kill anyone, Jed," Clint said. "Don't let my reputation influence your thinking. I'm out here to get my horse back."

Jed nodded, fell silent and continued on, studying the ground as he went.

Clint hated killing, and he wanted to believe what he had just told Jed; so how come everytime he thought of Moose Chandler, and the three men who had taken Duke away from him, his right hand itched?

And how come only the thought of his gun seemed to ease the itch?

THIRTY-ONE

Turk stood up on the ridge, matching stares with the black horse he knew as Devil. He was aware that behind him his three "partners" were having a discussion. He hoped that Roy Watson was explaining to them why they had to keep their killer instincts in check for a while. It was either that, or they were discussing how to get rid of Turk, and if that were the case, he'd have to kill the three of them, and he was hoping to avoid that . . . just now.

His thoughts moved on to Clint Adams, and to what he had seen in Adams's hotel room the other morning: Gail, Moose's daughter, in the Gunsmith's bed. If he had told Chandler about that, the old man would have gone after Clint Adams with a gun—and gotten himself killed. Moose Chandler wouldn't do Matt Turquette any good dead. Maybe later, after Adams was dead, Turk would tell Chandler, just to see the look on his face.

Gail was another story. She wasn't the most beautiful woman he'd ever seen, but she was a big girl, and that was the kind of woman Turk needed. She never paid any attention to

THE PANHANDLE SEARCH 139

Turk, though. He was just her father's hired hand, but that would change once he killed the Gunsmith.

Matt Turquette wouldn't be anyone's hired hand ever again, not after that.

"He ain't moved yet, huh?" Watson asked, coming up alongside Turk.

"He's had no reason to," Turk said. "When we make a move towards him, he'll take that herd and clear out."

"You sure know your horses, don't you, Turk?"

Turk looked at Watson and said, "I know more than horses, Roy. I know how certain types of people think, too."

"Is that because you're the same type?"

"I commanded a lot of men in the army, Roy," Turk said, "a lot of different types of men. I know how to handle them."

"Is that a fact?"

"Yeah, it is," Turk said, turning so that he faced Watson squarely, "and don't forget it."

Turk was at least eight inches taller than Watson, but his size didn't seem to intimidate the smaller man.

"You impress me, Roy," Turk said. "I think maybe you and I could get along."

"Without them, you mean?" Roy asked.

"Well, they're here now," Turk said. "What was that little powwow about?"

"I just told the boys to stay in line and keep their hands off their guns until they hear different."

"From you, or me?" Turk asked.

"That doesn't really make a difference, does it, Turk?" Watson asked.

Turk hesitated a moment, then said, "As long as they do as they're told, I guess it doesn't matter—just make sure that they do, though."

"They will," Watson said, "but they'll be looking to get something out of it."

"Reputations as the men who killed the famous Gunsmith," Turk said. "That could carry us a long way, Roy."

"That could get us killed, Turk," Watson countered. "I'm talking about money."

"You want money?" Turk asked. "Fine, I'll get you money, and I'll take the credit for killing Adams."

"You can have it," Watson said. "I don't need any reputation-hunting kids coming after me with a gun."

"Fine," Turk said. "Then we agree."

"I've got one thing to say to you, Turk," Watson said.

"What?"

"I want to warn you. We'll help you with Adams, but when the time comes for us to get our share, you'd better not try to hold out."

"Why would I do that?"

"I don't know why," Watson said. "Just don't."

"Roy, I've broken men in half with my hands for talking to me like that," Turk said.

"That's very interesting," Watson said. "Maybe you'd better concentrate on taking your own advice, then."

"What do you mean?"

"Control yourself, Turk," Watson said, "until after this is all over."

Mentally, Turk backed off a bit. Let Roy Watson say whatever he wanted to say now. Turk's time would come later, after he didn't need One-Eye Doran, Lefty Barron or Roy Watson anymore.

Gail Chandler realized that she had her mother's stubborn streak and impulsiveness. That was what had gotten her out

THE PANHANDLE SEARCH 141

here in the middle of nowhere, riding around trying to find either Turk or Clint Adams.

What made her think she could find them when she didn't even know what they were out here looking for?

It was her father's fault. She was able to control those dubious attributes she'd inherited from her mother in everyone else's company, but when it came to her father . . . He always seemed to know what to say or do to set her off.

So she was stuck out here, hoping against hope that she would run into Clint Adams. Was he really the Gunsmith? If so, why hadn't he told her? Was he afraid of how she would feel towards a man with a reputation?

How could he be such a man, though? He was so kind and gentle when she was with him. How could that kind of man also be the kind of man the Gunsmith was supposed to be?

She wanted him to explain that almost as much as she wanted to warn him about Turk.

She remembered the way Turk used to look at her when she lived on the ranch. That had driven her away almost as much as her father had. Turk was an animal, and what was worse, he probably had some men with him. What chance would Clint have against them?

For the first time since speaking to her father, she hoped that Clint *was* the Gunsmith. At least that would give him a better chance of surviving.

Moose Chandler knew where he was headed, because he—like Turk—knew horses. He wasn't out there trying to catch up to his daughter, he was trying to get there ahead of her.

Damn fool girl.

In spite of the circumstances that had gotten him on horseback, Chandler was enjoying the opportunity to get out and ride hard. Prior to the trip that started this whole mess, he had done very little work outside of his office. The trip had given him the chance to get out again, and it had been invigorating—and tiring. He was too old to be getting out on horseback too often, but an occasional ride was going to be a must in the future. As a horseman, when his time came to die, he wanted to do it in the saddle.

But he didn't want to do it today. Today, he wanted this problem solved, and done with. It was just as well that Gail had come out here, causing him to follow her, because now he'd be in on it at the end. He'd see it finished, one way or the other, and then get on with business.

He'd learned a lesson from this: Don't steal what you can't buy, and if you do, make sure the man you're stealing it from is nobody.

Still, even though that devil of a horse was a gelding, and couldn't be used for breeding purposes, what a glorious thing it would have been to be able to ride him.

THIRTY-TWO

"There they are," Jed said, triumphantly. He was pointing down into a valley that existed between two ridges, but Clint wasn't looking there.

"Hold up, Jed."

"But the herd is there. Can you see your horse from here?" he asked, excitedly.

"Not yet," Clint said.

"You're not even looking."

"I'm looking up on that ridge, Jed," Clint said, inclining his head in that direction.

"Why?"

"Because there's someone up there," he answered. "I caught a flash of movement, and something shiny."

"Like what?"

"Like the sun reflecting off a man's shiny belt—or a shiny gun," Clint said.

"Is it Turk?" Jed asked, anxiously. "How many men does he have with him?"

"I said I caught a flash, nothing more, Jed," Clint said. "The rest we've got to find out for ourselves."

"How?"

"We've got to get behind that ridge."

"But you won't be able to see the whole herd from there," Jed argued. "What if your horse is down there?"

"If he is, he'll wait," Clint said. "I'm not going to ride down there and find him just to get killed doing it. Can you get us around that ridge?"

"Sure," Jed said. "Come on."

Clint hesitated a moment, then, tempted just to take a peek down there, a quick look for Duke, but astride Lance, he'd be easy to spot a mile away. There were a lot of men alive who could hit with a gun anything they could see.

One of those men might just be up there on that ridge, and that wasn't worth a peek.

THIRTY-THREE

"How long are we going to wait up here?" Lefty Barron demanded out loud to anyone who would listen. "It's getting late, you know. It'll be dark soon."

"Stop complaining," Watson said.

"How about somebody else coming over here and watching these damned horses then," Lefty said. "That black is giving me the willies."

"Have you seen anyone yet?" Turk asked.

"No, I haven't seen anyone yet," Lefty said, "and I don't think I'm going to. I'm getting pretty tired of this."

Turk looked at Watson, who nodded, indicating that everything would be all right.

"Relieve him, One-Eye," Watson said. "Let him come back here and get some coffee."

Shaking his head, One-Eye Doran got to his feet and walked over to where Lefty Barron was seated.

"Go ahead, Lefty," One-Eye said.

"That black ain't human," Lefty said, rising, complaining under his breath.

One-Eye Doran sat down with his rifle across his knees and stared down at the horse who had bitten him on the hand. All he wanted to do was put a bullet between its eyes, and he was sure he could do it from right where he was.

"Look at him," Turk said to Watson. "He's dying to pull the trigger on that horse."

"He won't," Watson assured him. "Not yet, anyway."

"He'll get his chance," Turk said. "He can have the horse. I want the man."

Watson sat back against his saddle and chewed on a piece of beef jerky. One-Eye could have the horse, and Turk could have the man. All he knew was that he'd better come out of this with some money in his pocket, or he was going to be very unhappy.

And Roy Watson got real mean when he was unhappy.

It took the better part of twenty minutes for Jed to work them around to where they were behind the men on the ridge.

"Now what?"

"Now you sit tight and keep the horses quiet," Clint said, dismounting. "I'm going to take a walk up there and see how many men we're dealing with."

"You sure you don't want me to come with you?" Jed asked.

"I'll make less noise alone, Jed," Clint said. "Be patient and I'll be right back."

Jed watched as Clint worked his way up the steep incline, then grabbed both horses' reins and found himself a comfortable rock to sit and wait on. He hoped there were at least two or three men with Turk. This chance might never come again. He was actually going to get the opportunity to see the Gunsmith in action.

That was the same thing as seeing Wild Bill himself—if he was still alive.

He hoped nothing happened while he was down here waiting.

THIRTY-FOUR

Clint covered the distance between himself and whoever was on the ridge as quietly and swiftly as possible. His heart was pounding in his chest, because, for all he knew, Duke was just on the other side of this ridge, waiting for him.

As he was wondering how much farther he had to go, he suddenly heard voices.

"You know," one said, "I could hit any one of those horses right between the eyes from here. Why don't I just drop a few, to keep in practice?"

"You pull that trigger, Doran," a familiar voice said, "and I'll yank it off and make you eat it."

Clint was certain that it was the voice of Turk. And he was speaking to One-Eye Doran. Could Barron and Roy Watson be far?

Moving cautiously, Clint worked his way farther up the incline until he was able to look over the top.

Turk was unmistakable; even though he was sitting on the

THE PANHANDLE SEARCH 149

ground, he was obviously taller than a lot of men. There were three men on the ridge with him, two of whom Clint recognized.

The man with one hand was Lefty Barron, and seated between him and Turk was Roy Watson. They were the two who had braced him in the livery in Little Creek.

On the edge of the ridge with the rifle and eye patch was One-Eye Doran. Beyond those four, he couldn't see anyone else—but those four were enough. There were too many for him to step into sight and face them alone. He was going to have to do it some other way.

He backed down the incline until he was out of earshot, then turned and made his way quickly back down to the bottom, where Jed was waiting.

"What happened up there?" Jed asked anxiously.

"Nothing," Clint said. "There are four of them."

"Turk?"

"Yeah," Clint said, "and he's got Lefty, One-Eye and Roy Watson with him."

"Like we figured," Jed said.

"Yeah, just like we figured," Clint said.

"Well, what do we do now?" Jed said.

"Nothing, right now," Clint said.

"Don't you want me to go up there with you—" Jed started to say.

"No, Jed," Clint said, cutting him off. "I don't want you to go up there with me, now or later. I hired you as a guide, not for your gun."

"Aw, Clint—"

"Don't give me an argument, Jed," Clint said. "I'll give you something to do, but I'm going to keep you out of any shooting, if I can."

Jed fell silent, clearly dissatisfied with the way things had progressed. If he wasn't anywhere near the shooting, it meant he wouldn't get a chance to see the Gunsmith in action.

"Okay, Clint," he said. "Have it your way."

But Jed had no intention of giving up that easily.

THIRTY-FIVE

When darkness fell Clint said, "All right, I'm going back up, Jed."

"And what do I do?" Jed asked.

"I'm going to go three-quarters of the way up," Clint said, "and when I get there I'm going to signal—"

"How?"

"Let me finish. I'll signal you by lighting a match. After that I want you to walk your horse out about twenty yards or so, and then ride back as noisily as possible."

"But . . . they'll hear me."

"I want them to hear you," Clint explained. "One of them will probably come down to check."

"And what do I do when he gets here?"

"You won't have that problem," Clint said, "because he'll never get here."

Jed frowned, then brightened and said, "Oh!"

"Have you got it?"

"I've got it," Jed said. "Good luck."

"Watch for the signal."

"You can count on me."

"I hope so," Clint said. "After I signal you, make sure you stay down here."

"Sure, Clint," Jed said, "sure."

Clint studied Jed for a few moments, hoping that the boy would do what he was told, and then started up the hill. He moved even more slowly and quietly than before, because it was night now, and sounds carried better at night. That was how he knew that the men at the top of the ridge would hear Jed when he rode up, and at least one of them would have to go and check.

Finally, he arrived at what he felt was the three-quarter point. He took out a match, lit it and moved it back and forth, so that Jed couldn't miss it. When he doused the match, he listened carefully, to see if he could hear Jed walking his horse away, and found that he could not. After a few moments, he heard Jed's horse as he rode back up, and then flattened himself against the side of the hill.

"What was that?" he heard a voice call out.

"Sounded like a horse," Turk's voice said. "One of you go and check it out."

"What if it's—"

But that was all he heard. It was as if Turk had ordered everyone to keep their voices down.

Clint remained stock-still and listened intently. After a few seconds he heard sounds that indicated at least one man was on his way down. He heard the sound of a boot scraping stone, and then some loose stones tumbling down the hill. As the sounds came closer he got ready, hand hovering near his gun.

The moon was only a quarter full, and in its light he was unable to tell which man was approaching, but that didn't matter much. He was going to treat them all the same, anyway.

Whoever it was, he wasn't very observant, or perhaps he

was just intent on getting to the base of the hill, but he went right by Clint. Clint stood up quickly, moved in behind the man and pressed the barrel of his gun against the man's spine.

The man stiffened, and stopped.

"Don't make a sound," Clint said. "If you do, I'll blow a hole right through you."

The man remained quiet.

"Put your hands up."

The man obeyed. When Clint saw the empty cuff, he knew that the man was Lefty Barron.

"All right, Lefty," Clint said, removing the gun from Barron's holster, "let's continue down, slowly and quietly."

They walked down the hill, Clint prodding Barron in the back every so often with his gun barrel, just to remind him that he was there. They were almost to the bottom when they met Jed on his way up.

"What are you doing here?" Clint asked.

Wide-eyed, holding his rifle ahead of him, Jed said, "I thought you might need help."

"I told you to wait," Clint said.

"I thought you'd need help," Jed said again.

"Well, let's get him back down and we'll talk about it here," Clint said.

Barron stayed quiet while they worked their way down, and then said, "There's more of us up there, Adams. You're still outnumbered."

"I'm working at evening the odds, Barron," Clint said. "Tie his hands, Jed."

Jed stared and said, "He ain't got but one!"

"Then tie his wrists," Clint amended. "Just make sure he can't get loose."

"And then what?"

"Then you stay here with him while I go back up."

"You want me to make some more noise?"

"No," Clint said and, looking at Barron, added, "And if *he* does, blow a hole in him."

"You bet," Jed said, enthusiastically. Clint didn't rightfully know if the kid could do it, but then Barron didn't look so sure, himself.

"You ain't gonna make it through the night, Adams," Barron said.

"Well, if I don't," Clint replied, "you won't, either. That's a promise." He looked at Jed and said, "Make sure you keep him quiet."

"Yessir."

Jed trained his rifle on the trussed-up Barron and watched Clint start back up the slope. As soon as Clint faded into the darkness, Jed moved towards Barron, with a particular intention in mind.

Gail Chandler sat at her fire, cursing her father and mother, Turk, Clint Adams and anyone else she could think of. She wasn't lost. She knew exactly where she was, because she had grown up on this land. The only thing was, she didn't know where Clint Adams was, and for all the good she was doing out there, she might just as well have been lost.

She tested the air with her nose, but the only coffee she could smell was coming from her own camp. If Clint was out there somewhere, he was sitting in the dark—and so was Turk.

Damn, least they could have done was build a fire so she could find them.

Moose Chandler was walking his horse, wishing there was a full moon. He'd checked the valley nearest his house first and found it empty, although there were signs of a grazing herd that were about a day old. He had checked a few other places along the way and when darkness fell, he decided to

THE PANHANDLE SEARCH

keep riding. He was heading for another valley he knew about that lay between two high ridges. It was a perfect spot for a herd to spend the night, and an even better spot for an ambush.

If Turk was thinking the way he was thinking, and there was a herd in that valley, Turk would be waiting up on one of those ridges. The best place for Adams to look for his horse was among other horses. Oh, Moose knew that the leader of any herd would fight to keep that devil of a black horse away, but he also figured that Devil would take over any herd he wanted to in no time.

Chandler decided to saddle up and ride the rest of the way to that valley. He only hoped that he got there before the shooting started—and before Gail got there.

THIRTY-SIX

When Clint had climbed to within easy earshot he settled down on his belly and gave a listen.

"What the hell is keeping Lefty?" a man's voice said. It belonged to either Doran or Watson, because he would have recognized Turk.

"Why don't you go and check?" Turk asked.

"Why don't you stay where you are?" Roy Watson spoke up then, and Clint winced. Watson sounded like he had something on his mind.

"What are you talking about?" Doran asked.

"If Lefty don't come back, then chances are he ain't coming back," Watson said.

"You figure Adams is down there?" Turk asked.

"I don't know," Watson said, "but I ain't figuring on climbing down there in the dark to find out."

"You mean if Lefty don't come back, you ain't going after him?" One-Eye Doran demanded.

"I mean I ain't moving off this ridge until first light, and neither are you," Watson said.

THE PANHANDLE SEARCH

"If it was me down there—" Doran started, but Watson cut him off.

"I'd be doing the same thing," Watson said. "We ride together, One-Eye, but we ain't joined at the hip, and we ain't brothers. Fact is, I wouldn't go up against the Gunsmith in the dark even for my brother—if I had one."

Damn, Clint thought. If not for Watson, Doran and maybe even Turk might have come down for a look. Watson was the one with the brains, then, and the one to worry about. Turk may have thought he was the ramrod of the outfit, but Clint heard different.

"You mean you think the Gunsmith is behind us," Turk spoke up, "and we should just sit here and wait for daylight?"

"That's right."

"What's to stop him from coming up here and picking us off?" Doran asked.

"The same thing that's keeping us up here," Watson said. "The darkness."

"Wait a minute," Doran said. "Who's to say he ain't down there in that valley and we can't see him?"

"That herd of horses says so," Watson said. "Do you think they'd be standing so quiet if there was a man down there among them?"

"Roy's right, One-Eye," Turk said. "We've got to stay right where we are."

"And we might as well build a fire and keep warm," Watson said. "If he knows we're up here, there can't be any harm in it."

"What if he don't know?" Doran asked.

"He got one of us to go down there, didn't he?" Watson asked. "He's down there."

"Maybe Lefty will come back soon," Doran said.

"If he ain't back yet, he ain't coming back," Watson said.

"You think he's dead?" Doran asked.

"I think we'll find out come morning," Watson said. "Build a fire and make some coffee, One-Eye. I'm getting kind of cold."

That was it, then. Clint had gotten one man out of the way, but the other three were staying put for the night. Well, at least he knew where Turk and the others were, that was something.

He started back down the hill, with intentions of building a small fire of his own. He could use some coffee himself.

THIRTY-SEVEN

"How about letting me have some coffee?" Lefty Barron asked.

"That would mean untying you," Clint said, pouring himself a second cup.

"Don't tell me the Gunsmith is afraid of a man with one hand," Barron said.

"I'm careful around snakes, too, Lefty," Clint said, "and they don't have any hands."

Barron made a disgusted sound and looked over to where Jed was sitting, rifle across his knees and eyes up the slope, just in case somebody decided to slip down.

"Hey, kid, how about some coffee?"

Jed looked at him, and then looked away.

"I worked with that kid," Barron said in disgust.

"And you rode him, too," Clint said. "You don't have any friends here, Lefty. You might just as well keep your mouth shut and let some of that hot air keep you warm."

Barron stared at Clint Adams with hatred in his eyes, and then looked up the slope and wondered where his "friends" were. Why hadn't they come down to see where he got to?

"Nobody's coming down that slope in the dark, Lefty," Clint said, reading his mind. "There ain't nobody up there in that much of a hurry to die . . . not for you."

"We'll see who's gonna die, Adams," Barron said. "We'll see."

Clint took a swallow of the coffee and peered up the slope himself.

That feeling was in the air, all right. The feeling that, yeah, somebody was going to die.

One-Eye Doran looked down the slope and spotted the glow of a fire from behind some rocks.

"Roy, we could sneak on down there and—"

"Get away from there, One-Eye," Roy called out. "You sneak down there and you'll never sneak anywhere else."

"We gotta do something," Doran said. "Lefty's down there, maybe dead."

"If he's dead, there's nothing you can do for him," Turk said, "and if he's alive, he'll still be there come morning."

"Damn!" Doran said. He walked back to the edge and looked down to where he knew the horses were. "If we had a decent moon, I could plug that horse of his right now."

"Sit down and relax, One-Eye," Turk said. "You're gonna need all your strength in the morning."

"We gonna kill him in the morning?" Doran asked.

"We'll do what we have to do, One-Eye," Roy said. "Why don't you get some coffee?"

One-Eye walked to the fire to pour himself some coffee, and Watson walked over to where Turk was seated on the ground.

"You know," he said, "there's another way to look at this situation."

"How's that?" Turk asked.

"Is there another way down from this ridge?" Watson asked.

Turk thought a moment, then said, "Not an easy one. Why, you thinking of working around behind him?"

"That occurred to me," Watson said, "but something else also occurred to me."

"Like what?"

"Like we came out here as the hunters," Watson said, "and now it looks like we're the hunted."

"How do you figure that?"

"We're up here and he's down there," Watson said. "He can just sit and wait for us to try and come down."

"And if we don't?"

Watson laughed.

"We ain't outfitted for the long haul, Turk," Watson reminded him. "We got to run short of supplies some time, and he knows it."

"Well, we can try going down the other side, but the horses wouldn't make it."

Watson looked up at the sky and said, "Well, we've got a few hours yet before we have to make a decision. We might as well get some rest. I'll have One-Eye stand watch."

"Right," Turk said.

As Watson walked over to One-Eye, it occurred to him that he had lost control of this situation. Watson was the man taking charge, but if they got out of this alive, that was okay with him. When it was over, he'd step in and take charge again. Watson might be smarter, but Turk was bigger and stronger, and probably faster, and you needed more than smart to kill a man.

Didn't you?

* * *

J.R. ROBERTS

"What's going on?" One-Eye Doran asked when Watson came up alongside him.

"We might be in a little trouble here, One-Eye," Watson said, "but if you do what I say, we can ride it out."

"What about Turk?" Doran asked.

"We'll take care of Turk, too," Watson said.

"And Lefty?"

"Don't worry about Lefty," Watson said, "he can take care of himself. Our problem will be getting off this ridge in the morning. Just follow my lead, and we'll make it."

"I want a shot at that horse, first," One-Eye said, flexing his injured hand. "I owe him."

"Well, you're gonna have to decide what you want to do more," Watson said, "kill that horse . . . or live."

"All right," Clint told Jed, "I'll take over. You get some sleep."

"I can stay awake," Jed assured him.

"I'm going to need you in the morning, Jed," Clint explained, "and I want you well rested."

"What about him?" Jed asked, indicating Lefty Barron.

"Did you tie him tightly?"

"Of course."

"Then he'll be fine," Clint said. "Just go over and check his ropes, and then get some sleep."

"Check his ropes?" Jed asked. "But you just asked me—"

"I know," Clint said, "but it always pays to be on the safe side."

Jed went over to Barron, who was dozing, and yanked on the ropes that secured his wrists and ankles.

"What the hell are you doing?" Barron demanded.

"Double-checking," Jed said. "Now go to sleep and get some rest, or I'll blow a hole in you."

Jed went over to his bedroll to lie down, and Barron looked over at Clint, who just shrugged.

"I guess I created a monster," he said.

THIRTY-EIGHT

At first light Clint woke Jed so they could both be on the alert.

"Can I make breakfast?" Jed asked.

"It's already made," Clint said, handing him a piece of jerky. "I got up early, just for you."

"Thanks a lot," Jed said, taking it. "What about coffee?"

"Just what's left from last night."

"Great."

"Hey," Barron called, "what about me?"

"What about you?" Clint asked.

"My circulation is cut off," the man complained. "My hand is getting numb."

"You'll be okay," Clint assured him.

"What are we going to do now?" Jed asked. "Go up after them?"

"I don't see why," Clint said. "They've got to come down sometime. We can just wait them out."

"There is another way down, you know," Jed said, chewing on a piece of dried beef.

"No, I didn't know," Clint said. "That's why I brought you along, remember?"

"Well, it's not an easy way down," Jed pointed out. "In fact, if they came down that way, they wouldn't be able to bring their horses."

"That's no good, then," Clint said, "because they wouldn't leave themselves on foot."

"If you say so."

"No," Clint said, looking up the slope and squinting against the glare of the rising sun, "they've got to come down sometime, and we'll be waiting."

"What about the horses?" Jed said. "What about *your* horse? They won't stay in that valley forever."

"That's true," Clint said, "but if Duke is with them, at least I know he's safe."

"And if he's not with them?"

"Then I'll just have to keep looking," Clint said, "after we finish up here."

"It's morning," Watson said, nudging One-Eye awake with the toe of his boot. "Get up."

One-Eye sat up, squinting his one eye and asked, "Did Lefty get back?"

"No, he's not back yet," Watson said. "The coffee's ready."

One-Eye looked over at the fire, where Turk squatted, pouring himself a cup of coffee.

One-Eye Doran got to his feet and he and Watson walked over to the fire.

"Well, what are we gonna do?" Doran asked when they all had coffee cups in their hands.

"Well," Watson said, looking at Turk—they had talked it over before waking Doran, and had agreed on a course of action—"Turk says there's another way down from here. You're gonna take it," Watson said.

"And work behind him?" Doran said. "I'll go for that. Let me saddle my horse—"

"That's the problem," Watson said. "You'll have to go down on foot. A horse would be too much of a problem."

"You want me to work my way down on foot?"

"We'll saddle your horse and have him ready for you," Turk promised. "Once you get behind him, we'll start down while you keep him busy."

"When we get to the bottom, there'll be too many of us for him to handle," Watson said.

Doran thought it over, and it seemed to make sense to him, only because it was Watson's idea as much as Turk's. In fact, it was probably Roy's idea from the start, and he conned Turk into thinking he was in on it.

"When do I start?" he asked, looking at Watson and pointedly ignoring Turk.

"Right now," Turk said.

Doran kept his eye on Watson, who nodded and said, "Yeah, now would be a good time, One-Eye."

"Okay," Doran said, dumping the remains of his coffee into the fire. "All I need is two seconds to finish off that horse."

He got up and crossed over to his rifle, but Watson was right behind him.

"Forget the horse," he said, grabbing Doran by the arm and spinning him around.

"I want my shot at that horse, Roy!"

"You'll get it," Watson said, "when I say so, Orville."

One-Eye's one eye narrowed and he said, "Don't call me that, Roy."

"Then stop acting dumb," Watson said. "I don't know

THE PANHANDLE SEARCH

what Adams is doing right now, but if he's sleeping a shot will wake him up."

"He ain't gonna be sleeping—" Doran started to say, but he stopped himself as he realized what Watson meant. With a yearning look down into the valley he said, "Look at him."

Watson looked down and saw the big black standing straight and tall, and damned if he didn't look like he was looking right up there.

"Look at him just standing there," Doran said. "Why doesn't he take them and move?"

"Maybe he's waiting," Watson said.

"Yeah," Doran said, looking at his rifle. "Well, I just hope he waits a little bit longer."

"He'll be there, One-Eye," Watson said, making it sound like a promise. "After we finish with Adams, he's all yours."

"Yeah," Doran said. He picked up his rifle and said, "How long is it supposed to take me to get down there?"

"Depends on how fast you can go," Watson said, "but we'll give you an hour and then we'll move. When you see us you better start shooting."

"What if I don't have a clear shot?"

"Start shooting anyway."

"Okay," Doran said. He turned to go, then turned back and said, "What if I get down there and the hour's not up and I *have* a clear shot?"

Watson poked Doran in the chest with his finger. "If you can put Adams away, One-Eye, you do it."

"What about Turk?" Doran said. "He wants to pull the trigger on Adams."

"Don't worry about Turk," Watson said. "If you put Adams away, I'll put Turk away. It's that simple."

THIRTY-NINE

"I just thought of something," Clint said. He was starting a fresh pot of coffee and Jed was sitting with his eyes on the slope.

"What's that?"

"That other way down you told me about."

"They wouldn't be able to bring their horses," Jed reminded him.

"I know that," Clint said, "but one of them could come down while the other two stayed up there."

"And work his way around behind us, you mean?" Jed asked, turning his eyes away from the slope.

"Which way would he come from?" Clint asked.

"There," Jed said, pointing to Clint's right.

"All right," Clint said, putting the coffeepot down and forgetting about it. "You keep your eyes on that slope, and at the first sign of trouble give a holler. I'm going to take a short walk and see what I can see."

"If one of them started down at first light, he should be just about down by now," Jed warned. "Be careful."

"You too."

THE PANHANDLE SEARCH   169

Clint started working his way to his right, and soon Jed and the trussed-up Lefty Barron were out of sight. Why hadn't he thought of this before? For all he knew he could be under someone's gun right now.

With a constant itch on his back—right where the center of a bull's-eye would be if one had been drawn on the back of his shirt—he continued to work swiftly and quietly along the base of the slope, which was becoming steeper and steeper with each step.

One-Eye Doran had had a hair-raising trip down, but he was almost to the bottom. If he'd had two eyes, and the advantage of peripheral vision in each, he would have seen the Gunsmith much sooner than he did. It was not until he had both feet on the ground that he turned to his left and saw Clint Adams standing about ten feet away from him.

Jesus, he said to himself.

"Hello, One-Eye," Clint greeted.

"Adams."

"The back of my head remembers you well, Doran," Clint told him.

"I can explain that," Doran said nervously. He hadn't expected to have to *face* the Gunsmith on his own, and he was justifiably frightened.

"I'm sure you can," Clint said. "You were only trying to take my head off, right?"

"Look," Doran said, "it wasn't my idea. I didn't want the damn horse, Chandler did."

"You admit that you stole my horse for Chandler?"

"Why else would we take it?"

"Who's we?"

"You know who," Doran said.

"I want you to tell me."

"I can't do that, Adams," Doran said.

"Then we're at a stand-off," Clint said. "You're going to have to make a move, Doran."

"Now, wait a minute—"

"Either that, or give me some names."

Doran stared at Clint for a while, flexing and unflexing his left hand, which was bandaged, and his right one, which was his gun hand.

"All right, all right, wait a minute," he finally said. "It was me, Roy Watson and Lefty Barron." Doran narrowed his eyes then and asked, "Did you kill Lefty?"

"Lefty's fine," Clint said, "and you will be too, as long as you unbuckle that gunbelt and let it fall to the ground, nice and easy."

"How do I know you won't kill me, anyway?"

"You don't," Clint said, and waited while the man made his decision.

"Just give me a chance to think," Doran complained.

"If you stop to think, One-Eye, you're going to end up getting killed," Clint said. "Just do what I told you to do."

"Damn," Doran said through his teeth. Now he wished he had plugged that horse before he came down here. At least he would have gotten that done.

"Drop the gun or grab it, Doran," Clint said.

One-Eye Doran's bandaged hand was moving for the belt buckle when the shot sounded behind Clint. Almost distracted because he knew Jed was alone, Clint's eyes flicked away from One-Eye Doran for a split second. During that split second, Doran changed his mind.

He decided to die.

FORTY

Clint saw One-Eye's unbandaged hand had start moving towards his gun and knew that the man had made the wrong decision. He didn't have time to be fancy and try wounding Doran, because he had to get back to where he left Jed, so he simply drew and fired faster than One-Eye's eye could follow.

The first slug punched Doran through the chest, and the second took out his throat as he was slumping to the floor. Keeping his gun in his hand Clint turned and ran back the way he had come.

As he ran he heard several more shots, and was sure that they were coming from different guns. From the sound of it, Jed was involved in a firefight, and Clint quickened his pace.

As he arrived on the scene he was surprised to find that not only was the kid involved in a firefight, but that he was stuck in a crossfire. Turk and Watson had come down the ledge and finding whatever cover they could had started firing at Jed. There was also gunfire coming from a stand of brush behind their camp, but Clint could not see who was doing the shooting. He was willing to guess, though, being reasonably sure that he'd be right.

His guess was Moose Chandler.

"What the hell happened to Doran?" Turk shouted to Watson.

"Maybe that's him, firing from that brush," Watson called back.

"That's not One-Eye," Turk said.

"How do you know that?"

"Because just as he started firing, I saw who it was," Turk replied.

"Oh, yeah?" Watson said. "Who?"

"That's Moose."

"Chandler?" Watson asked, looking away from what he was doing. "What the hell is he doing here?"

"I don't know, but what I'd like to know is what happened to Adams."

As he asked, he saw Clint Adams coming from the other direction, and called out, "There he is!"

Watson looked to where he was pointing and they both stopped firing at the kid and started firing at the Gunsmith.

As the hail of bullets rained down from the slope, Clint threw himself to the ground and crawled the rest of the way to Jed, who was crouched down behind his saddle.

"What happened?" he asked. "Are you all right?"

"I'm fine," Jed said, "but we're pinned down. They started shooting from the slope, and then someone started firing from behind me. It must be Doran."

"It's not," Clint said. "My guess is it's Moose Chandler."

"Mr. Chandler?" Jed asked, looking surprised. "What brought him out here?"

THE PANHANDLE SEARCH

"He probably wants to be in on the finish," Clint said. He fired twice up the slope and scattered some stone splinters in Roy Watson's face.

"What are we gonna do?" Jed asked, firing back towards the brush. "What happened to One-Eye?"

"He's dead."

"With Lefty tied up, that should have cut the odds in half," Jed said. "Why do I feel like we're still in bad trouble?"

They scattered to put more space between them as another hail of lead came down off the slope.

"Jesus, don't those guys ever have to reload?" Jed demanded.

"Actually, you're right," Clint said, "they do have to reload, and so does the man in that brush, whether it's Moose or not."

"You got an idea?"

"Yes," Clint said. He reached over his saddle and snatched up his rifle just ahead of a couple of chunks of lead.

"You keep firing up the slope and keep them ducking," Clint said. "As soon as there's a pause from the brush, that's where I'm headed. If we can get rid of him, we'll be more in control of the situation."

"All right," Jed said, "but I hope you can outrun flying lead."

"I'm counting on you to keep that flying lead down to a minimum," Clint said.

"That ain't what you hired me for," Jed reminded him.

"I'll pay extra," Clint said.

"I hope I live to collect," Jed said.

Clint reloaded his hand gun, and then commenced firing into the brush with his rifle, spacing his shots out. Jed did the same as he fired up the slope.

Suddenly, Clint's chance was there. The firing from the brush had stopped.

"This is it!" Clint said. "Start firing!"

"Right."

Jed increased his rate of fire and Clint stood up in a crouch and started running toward the stand of brush. As he approached it, however, he saw the barrel of a rifle poke through, and he wasn't sure he was going to make it in time.

Gail Chandler had just about given up any hope of finding Clint when she heard the shots.

"Oh, my God," she said to herself, and spurred her horse into a gallop, toward where she thought the shots were coming from.

Clint knew he'd never make the last few steps, so he braced himself for the impact of the bullets and hurled himself through the air and into the brush.

As he landed he felt the barrel of the gun strike his side, and then it went off. He rolled and struck the gunman with his entire body. They both went over from the impact, Clint holding onto his gun, but the other man's rifle went flying from his grasp.

There was a clearing inside the stand of brush, and that was where Clint found himself as he stopped rolling. He came up on one knee with his gun held out in front of him, just as Moose Chandler righted himself and clawed for his own sidearm.

"I wouldn't, Moose," he warned, and Chandler froze. "Did you decide to be in on the finish?"

"You scum," Chandler said. "You'd use a man's own daughter against him."

"What the hell are you talking about?" Clint demanded.

"You know damn well—"

THE PANHANDLE SEARCH

"Let's talk about that later, Moose," Clint said. "Right now you'd better order those men down from the slope, without their guns."

"They wouldn't listen to me," Chandler said.

"Why not? You're their boss, aren't you? This is your fight, isn't it?"

"I have a feeling Turk might have his own stake in this," Chandler said.

"Well, why don't we find out?" Clint asked. "Let's go."

"I'm not stepping out into the open," Moose said. "That kid will put a bullet into me."

"It wouldn't be the worst thing he's ever done," Clint said, "but I'll protect you, Moose. Let's go."

"What the hell—" Turk said.

"What?" Watson asked, and Turk pointed to where Clint and Moose were stepping out into the open.

Down at the base of the slope, Jed was also staring at the two men stepping out from the brush.

"Hold your fire," Clint Adams called out.

"What's going on?" Watson wondered aloud.

"Let's give a listen," Turk said.

"Turk!" Moose Chandler called out. "You and whoever you got with you better throw down your weapons and come on down."

"Is he kidding?" Watson asked.

"I guess he still thinks he's the boss," Turk said. "You know, I used to respect that man, and even be a little afraid of him, but the way he's reacted to this whole thing kind of opened my eyes. He's no better than you or me, you know?"

"I know that," Watson said. He raised his rifle and sighted down the slope.

"What are you gonna do?" Turk asked.

"I'm gonna show him who the boss is, now," Watson

said. He fired once, and saw the slug strike Moose Chandler in the left shoulder.

"One more should do it," Watson said, and fired again.

When the first bullet hit Moose, Clint threw himself against the man, knocking him to the ground, just as the second bullet whizzed by.

Grabbing Moose under the shoulders he dragged him back into the brush, just as a few bullets kicked up some dust around them.

"I told you, damn it," Chandler hissed. "I told you that fool kid would shoot me."

"I've got news for you, Moose," Clint said. "The kid didn't shoot you, your own men did."

"What?"

"Those shots came from up the slope."

"But why?"

"I guess that's something you'll have to ask them, as soon as I get them down."

Clint looked at Moose's wound, which was bleeding a lot, but it looked like the bullet went clean through without hitting anything vital.

"You better just clamp your hand over that and stay put," Clint said. He picked up Chandler's handgun and tucked it into his belt, and then threw the rifle into the bushes where it lay, empty.

"What are you gonna do now?" Chandler asked.

"I'm going to get those two down from the slope," Clint said, "and then I'm taking my horse back."

"You can have him," Chandler said. "He's been more trouble than he's worth."

"I could have told you that right from the beginning," Clint said, "if you had asked me, but no, you had to steal him and find out the hard way."

"Yeah," Moose Chandler said, pressing his hand against

THE PANHANDLE SEARCH

his wound. The pain it was causing him was etched on his face, and he looked years older.

Clint was about to step out into the open again when he heard the sound of a horse approaching.

"Now what?" he wondered.

Suddenly, Gail was there, riding right into the middle of the firefight.

"Damn it, Gail," he said aloud.

"What?" Chandler demanded. Clutching his wound he moved next to Clint so he could see.

"Gail!" he shouted. "That's my daughter!"

Clint stared at Chandler, then at Gail and said, "I'll be damned."

FORTY-ONE

"She'll be killed!"

"Why—" Clint asked, but the firing started again and Gail's horse reared and dumped her on her behind. Whether it was by accident or design, she could very well have gotten killed out there, so he ran out to get her and became a target himself.

"Clint," she shouted when she saw him.

"Let's go, Gail," he said, grabbing her by the arms. He couldn't fire back at the moment, and had to count on Jed for cover.

He half dragged her back to the cover of the brush and pushed her in ahead of him.

"Father," she said when she saw Moose Chandler.

"Gail, why—"

"You're hurt!" she said, and went to him.

"You two have your reunion," Clint said. "I've got other things to do."

"I don't understand what's going on," Gail complained.

"There's a few things I don't understand myself," Clint

THE PANHANDLE SEARCH 179

said. "Your father can fill you in on a lot of it. I have to go."

"Go where—?" she started to ask, but he was gone.

"Something's wrong here," Watson said. "One-Eye must be dead, and Lefty's down there tied up—"

"And now you shot Moose," Turk said, "which was a brilliant move—and you tried to shoot Gail, and if we didn't need each other, I'd shoot you right now."

"Who is she, anyway?"

"That's Moose's daughter."

"You interested?"

"There's Adams," Turk said, and started shooting again. Watson joined in, but Clint was veering from side to side, presenting a difficult target.

"I thought you could shoot," Watson demanded.

"If he'd stand still, he'd be dead," Turk said.

"Well, he's not going to stand still, damn it," Watson said. "Turk, this party is over and I'm getting out."

"Where are you going?"

"Back to the horses," Watson said. "I'm getting on my horse and riding out of here."

"How?"

"Right through there," Watson said. "Adams wants his horse, so I'm going to leave it to him. I think once I'm past him he'll forget about me."

"If you get past him," Turk said.

"I'll get past him."

"What about Lefty and One-Eye?"

"They're grown men," Watson said. "They knew what they were getting into when they agreed to take on the Gunsmith."

"Go then," Turk said. "I'll finish it myself."

"That's what I thought," Watson said.

"What?"

J.R. ROBERTS

"You're *not* smart enough to know when to quit," Watson said. He turned his back on Turk and started up the slope. Turk was tempted to put one in Watson's back, but had a second thought. A more suitable time and place would arise very soon.

He turned his attention down the slope, where Clint Adams was once again taking cover with the kid behind their saddles.

"Hey," Jed said as Clint dropped down beside him.

"What's wrong?"

"That's Watson, running back up the slope. What's he up to?"

"I don't know, but I have a feeling we'll find out soon," Clint said.

"It's quiet, isn't it?" Jed asked.

"Yeah," Clint said. He lifted his head up and Turk fired once.

"They've changed their tactics," Clint said.

"Maybe they just decided not to waste lead."

"That could be . . ." Clint said, but he wasn't so sure. "We can only wait and see. They're still in the same spot they were in before."

"Which is?"

Looking up the slope Clint answered, "They've got to come down sometime."

When Turk heard the sound of horses from behind he realized that something was wrong. Turning, he saw that not only was Watson riding down on *his* horse, but he was driving three other horses ahead of him: Barron's, Doran's . . . and his own.

"Damn you, Watson!" he shouted.

Watson was shouting at the horses and couldn't hear

Turk's voice, but he could imagine what the man was saying. *Sorry, Turk,* he thought, *but everybody's got to look out for themselves.*

As Watson rode by Turk and continued on down the slope, Turk sighted down on his back with his rifle and squeezed the trigger, which he had intended to do, anyway—only now, he had even more incentive, besides self-preservation.

The impact of the shot knocked Watson out of the saddle, and he tumbled end over end down the slope until he reached the bottom.

By that time, Turk was on his feet and heading for the top. He knew he was close to being finished, but before he let the Gunsmith win, he was going to do what One-Eye had been wanting to do all along.

Kill the Gunsmith's horse.

FORTY-TWO

Clint and Jed had to scamper out of the way to avoid being trampled by the four horses, and meanwhile their own horses, off to one side and out of the line of fire, reacted to the running horses by calling out to them and straining against their secured reins.

As the horses went by Clint became aware of the man who was rolling down the slope in the horse's wake.

"What have we here?" he said. "Quiet the horses down, Jed, before they get loose."

"What about—"

"I don't think there's going to be any more shooting," Clint said. "Go on."

Jed went to tend to the horses and Clint rushed over to the fallen man. He saw the wound in his back, and when he turned him over he saw that it was Roy Watson.

"Stealing a man's horse is a lot of trouble, Roy," he told the dead man. "I could have told you that."

Looking up the slope he said, "That leaves Turk," and saw Turk running up to the top. Did he have another horse there? He doubted that. And he couldn't be expecting to get away that way. He must have had something else on his mind.

"Oh, no," he said as it hit him, and he started up the slope. "I'm going after Turk," he shouted.

". . . careful . . ." he dimly heard Jed calling, but he was moving so fast he didn't hear the rest.

His heart was pounding in his chest because he felt that he knew what Turk was up to. It was all over for him, but he was looking for a way to hurt the Gunsmith, and what other way than killing his horse? Suddenly, the slope seemed to be much steeper than it had been during any time of the day or night, and he seemed to be moving in quicksand. He had to get to the top before Turk could fire down into the valley at Duke.

He had to.

When Turk reached the top he turned and looked down, spotting Clint Adams. He could have turned and fired at Adams, but there was too much of a chance of missing. He would rather shoot the black horse and be sure that whatever happened, the Gunsmith would remember tangling with Matt Turquette.

He picked up his rifle and walked to the edge of the ridge. There was the black, standing like he was made out of stone.

"Good-bye, horse," he said, and raised his rifle.

Clint's breath was rasping in his chest, but he pushed himself to move even faster. When he reached the top he saw Turk standing at the edge, sighting down his rifle.

"Turk!" he shouted.

His voice distracted Turk just enough. The foreman looked over at him, then hurriedly sighted down the rifle barrel again. Clint, still over the side, with just his head and shoulders showing, drew his gun, brought it up over the ledge, and fired just as Turk did.

Or a split second after.

Clint's shot took Turk right off the edge of the ridge, and he could hear the man screaming all the way down. By the time he climbed up and rushed to the edge to look down, the screaming had stopped.

He holstered his gun and took his first look down into the valley at the herd of horses, hoping that Duke would be there, and that this hadn't all been for nothing.

"Duke, if you aren't there—" he started to say aloud, but there was no need for him to finish, because Duke stood out from every other horse in the herd.

Clint put his hands on his hips and breathed a sigh of relief at the sight of him. Apparently, Turk had not been as good a shot as he had thought himself to be—either that or he had rushed it. Whatever the reason, he had missed and Duke was fine.

When the big horse saw Clint standing on the crest of the ridge, he reared up on his hind legs, pawed the air, and whinnied loudly. He was a sight to see among all of those wild horses, and Clint couldn't help but wonder if Duke hadn't taken to the life of a wild horse.

"Duke," Clint said aloud, "I hope you're resigning as leader of that herd and not just telling me to get lost."

At that point the big gelding began to nod his head, as if he'd heard what the Gunsmith had said—or sensed it.

"Stay right where you are, big boy," Clint said, "and I'll be right down."

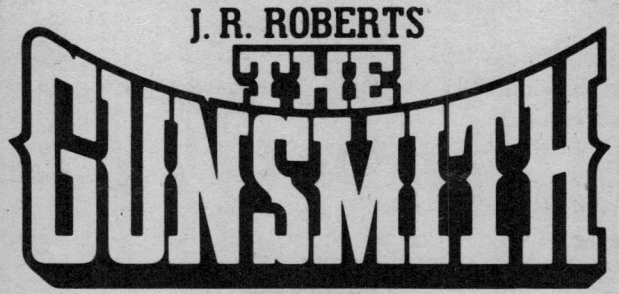

J. R. ROBERTS
THE GUNSMITH
SERIES

☐ 30928-3	THE GUNSMITH #1:	MACKLIN'S WOMEN	$2.50
☐ 30857-0	THE GUNSMITH #2:	THE CHINESE GUNMEN	$2.25
☐ 30858-9	THE GUNSMITH #3:	THE WOMAN HUNT	$2.25
☐ 30859-7	THE GUNSMITH #4:	THE GUNS OF ABILENE	$2.25
☐ 30925-9	THE GUNSMITH #5:	THREE GUNS FOR GLORY	$2.50
☐ 30861-9	THE GUNSMITH #6:	LEADTOWN	$2.25
☐ 30862-7	THE GUNSMITH #7:	THE LONGHORN WAR	$2.25
☐ 30901-1	THE GUNSMITH #8:	QUANAH'S REVENGE	$2.50
☐ 30864-3	THE GUNSMITH #9:	HEAVYWEIGHT GUN	$2.25
☐ 30924-0	THE GUNSMITH #10:	NEW ORLEANS FIRE	$2.50
☐ 30866-X	THE GUNSMITH #11:	ONE-HANDED GUN	$2.25
☐ 30926-7	THE GUNSMITH #12:	THE CANADIAN PAYROLL	$2.50
☐ 30927-5	THE GUNSMITH #13:	DRAW TO AN INSIDE DEATH	$2.50
☐ 30869-4	THE GUNSMITH #14:	DEAD MAN'S HAND	$2.25
☐ 30872-4	THE GUNSMITH #15:	BANDIT GOLD	$2.25

Prices may be slightly higher in Canada.

Available at your local bookstore or return this form to:

CHARTER BOOKS
Book Mailing Service
P.O. Box 690, Rockville Centre, NY 11571

Please send me the titles checked above. I enclose _____. Include 75¢ for postage and handling if one book is ordered; 25¢ per book for two or more not to exceed $1.75. California, Illinois, New York and Tennessee residents please add sales tax.

NAME_____

ADDRESS_____

CITY_____STATE/ZIP_____

(allow six weeks for delivery.) **A1/a**

J. R. ROBERTS
THE GUNSMITH
SERIES

☐ 30906-2	THE GUNSMITH #16: BUCKSKINS AND SIX-GUNS	$2.50
☐ 30907-0	THE GUNSMITH #17: SILVER WAR	$2.50
☐ 30908-9	THE GUNSMITH #18: HIGH NOON AT LANCASTER	$2.50
☐ 30909-7	THE GUNSMITH #19: BANDIDO BLOOD	$2.50
☐ 30891-0	THE GUNSMITH #20: THE DODGE CITY GANG	$2.25
☐ 30910-0	THE GUNSMITH #21: SASQUATCH HUNT	$2.50
☐ 30893-7	THE GUNSMITH #22: BULLETS AND BALLOTS	$2.25
☐ 30894-5	THE GUNSMITH #23: THE RIVERBOAT GANG	$2.25
☐ 30895-3	THE GUNSMITH #24: KILLER GRIZZLEY	$2.50
☐ 30896-1	THE GUNSMITH #25: NORTH OF THE BORDER	$2.50
☐ 30897-X	THE GUNSMITH #26: EAGLE'S GAP	$2.50
☐ 30899-6	THE GUNSMITH #27: CHINATOWN HELL	$2.50
☐ 30900-3	THE GUNSMITH #28: THE PANHANDLE SEARCH	$2.50
☐ 30902-X	THE GUNSMITH #29: WILDCAT ROUND-UP	$2.50

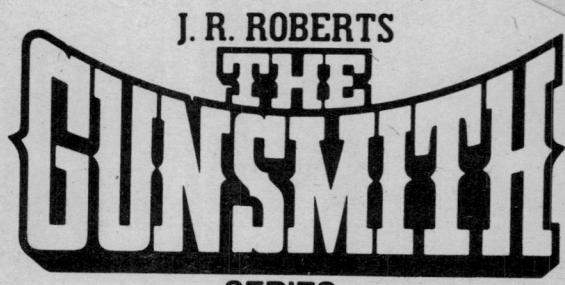

Prices may be slightly higher in Canada.

Available at your local bookstore or return this form to:

CHARTER BOOKS
Book Mailing Service
P.O. Box 690, Rockville Centre, NY 11571

Please send me the titles checked above. I enclose _____. Include 75¢ for postage and handling if one book is ordered; 25¢ per book for two or more not to exceed $1.75. California, Illinois, New York and Tennessee residents please add sales tax.

NAME _____

ADDRESS _____

CITY _____ STATE/ZIP _____

(allow six weeks for delivery.)

A1